PUFFIN BOOKS

Teddy Robinson Himself

Joan G. Robinson was born in Buckinghamshire in 1910. She studied at the Chelsea Illustrators' Studio and then went on to write and illustrate many books, of which the *Teddy Robinson* and *Mary-Mary* books are amongst the most well known. Joan Robinson was married with two daughters. She died in 1988.

Joan G. Robinson

TEDDY
ROBINSON
HIMSELF

PUFFIN BOOKS

PUFFIN BOOKS

Published by the Penguin Group
Penguin Books Ltd, 27 Wrights Lane, London W8 5TZ, England
Penguin Putnam Inc., 375 Hudson Street, New York,
New York 10014, USA
Penguin Books Australia Ltd, Ringwood, Victoria, Australia
Penguin Books Canada Ltd, 10 Alcorn Avenue, Toronto,
Ontario, Canada M4V 3B2
Penguin Books (NZ) Ltd, Cnr Rosedale and Airborne Roads, Albany,
Auckland, New Zealand

Penguin Books Ltd, Registered Offices: Harmondsworth,
Middlesex, England

First published in Great Britain by Harrap 1957
Published in Puffin Books with additional stories 1974
13 15 17 19 20 18 16 14

ADDITIONAL STORIES
'Teddy Robinson and the Mermaid' from *Another Teddy Robinson*
(Harrap, 1961); 'Teddy Robinson and the Band' from *More About
Teddy Robinson* (Harrap, 1954); 'Teddy Robinson and the Beautiful
Present' and 'Teddy Robinson Goes Magic' from *Teddy Robinson's
Book* (Harrap 1955) and 'Teddy Robinson and Guy Fawkes' from *Dear
Teddy Robinson* (Harrap, 1956)

Copyright © Joan G. Robinson, 1954, 1955, 1956, 1957, 1961, 1974
All rights reserved

Set in Monotype Imprint

Made and printed in England by Clays Ltd, St Ives plc

British Library Cataloguing in Publication Data
A CIP catalogue record for this book is available from
the British Library

ISBN 0–140–30752–4

For
Gregory
Barnaby
Mungo
Jessamy
*and everyone
who has a Teddy bear*

Contents

Contents

I

Teddy Robinson Goes to the Dancing-Class

TEDDY ROBINSON was a nice, big, comfortable, friendly teddy bear. He had light brown fur and kind brown eyes, and he belonged to a little girl called Deborah.

One Saturday morning Teddy Robinson saw that Deborah was putting on her best dress.

'Where are we going?' he said.

'To a dancing-class,' said Deborah, 'to learn to dance. Won't it be fun?'

'What, me?'

'Yes, you can come too. Will you like that?'

'I don't think I'd better dance,' said Teddy Robinson, 'but I shall like to come and watch.'

So he waited while Deborah put on her best socks and shoes, and had a red ribbon tied in her hair; then Deborah brushed his fur with the dolls' hair brush, and they were all ready to go.

'Oh, my shoes!' said Deborah. 'Where are they?'

'On your feet,' said Teddy Robinson, surprised.

'No, not these shoes,' said Deborah. 'I meant my dancing-shoes. I've got some new ones. They're very special – pink, with ribbons to keep them on.'

'Well I never!' said Teddy Robinson. 'You *have*

gone grand and grown-up. Fancy having special shoes to dance in!'

Mummy had the new shoes all ready in a bag.

'You can see them when we get there,' she said.

So they all set off. Mummy carrying the new shoes, Deborah hopping and skipping all the way, and Teddy Robinson singing to himself as he bounced up and down in her arms:

> 'Hoppity-skippity,
> rin-tin-tin –
> special shoes for dancing in,
> pink, with ribbons –
> well, fancy that!
> I'd dance myself if I wasn't so fat.'

When they got there Teddy Robinson stopped singing, and Deborah stopped hopping and skipping, and they followed Mummy into the cloakroom. Deborah changed into the new shoes, and had her hair brushed all over again; then they all went into the big hall.

Mary Jane was there, in a pale yellow dress with a frilly petticoat; and Caroline, with pink ribbons to match her party frock; and there was Andrew, in blue corduroy velvet trousers and shoes with silver buckles on them.

'Hallo, Teddy Robinson,' said Andrew. 'Have you come to dance?'

'Not today,' said Teddy Robinson. 'I didn't bring my shoes.'

'He is going to watch,' said Deborah, and she put

him down on an empty chair in the front row. Then she ran off to talk to Mary Jane and Caroline.

All the mothers and aunties and nurses who had come to watch the class were chatting together in the rows of chairs behind Teddy Robinson, and on the chair next to him sat a large walkie-talkie doll, wearing a pink frilled dress with a ribbon sash. She was sitting up very straight, smiling and staring in front of her.

Teddy Robinson wondered whether to speak to her, but just then a lady came in and sat down at the piano, and a moment later the teacher, whose name was Miss Silver, came into the hall.

Teddy Robinson decided he had better not start talking now, as the class was about to begin. Instead he listened to all the mothers and aunties and nurses, who had all begun talking to the children at once, in busy, whispering voices.

'Stand up nicely, point your toes.'

'Here's your hankie, blow your nose.'

'Don't be shy now, do your best. Make it up and follow the rest.'

'Where's your hankie? Did you blow?'

'There's the music. Off you go!'

Then the children all ran into the middle of the floor, and the dancing-class began.

Teddy Robinson, sitting tidily on his chair in the front row, thought how jolly it was to be one of the grown-ups who had come to watch, and how lucky he was to belong to the nicest little girl in the class.

'How pretty she looks in her new pink shoes and her

red ribbon,' he said to himself. 'And how well she can dance already! She is doing it quite differently from all the others. When they are doing *hop*, *one-two-three* she is doing *one-two-three*, *hop*, *hop*, *hop*, and it looks so much jollier that way. She is the only one able to do it right. None of the others can keep up with her.'

He smiled proudly as Deborah went dancing past, her eyes shining, her red ribbon flying.

A lady in the row behind whispered to someone else, 'Who is that little girl with the red ribbon, the one who hops three times instead of once?'

The other lady whispered back, 'I don't know. She is new, you can see that – but isn't she enjoying herself? That's her teddy bear on the chair in front.'

Teddy Robinson pretended he wasn't listening and hummed softly to himself in time to the music. He was pleased that other people had noticed Deborah too. He looked sideways at the walkie-talkie doll. She was still smiling, and watching the dancing carefully. Teddy Robinson was glad to think that she too was admiring Deborah.

When the music stopped and the children paused for breath Teddy Robinson turned to her.

'Aren't you dancing?' he asked.

'No,' said the doll; 'I walk and talk, but I don't dance. I've come to watch.'

'I've come to watch too,' said Teddy Robinson.

'I suppose you don't dance either?' said the doll, looking at Teddy Robinson's fat tummy.

'No, I sing,' said Teddy Robinson.

12

"Aren't you dancing?"

'Ah, yes,' said the doll, 'you have the figure for it.'

The children began dancing again, and the lady at the piano played such hoppity-skippity music that Teddy Robinson couldn't help joining in with a little song, very quietly to himself:

'Hoppity-skippity, one-two-three,
The bestest dancer belongs to me.
Oh, what a fortunate bear I be!
Hoppity-skippity, one-two-three.'

The walkie-talkie doll turned to Teddy Robinson.

'How beautifully she dances!' she said. 'I'm not surprised so many people have come to watch her.'

'Thank you,' said Teddy Robinson, bowing slightly,

13

and feeling very proud. 'Yes, she does dance well, and this is her first lesson.'

'Oh, no, it's not,' said the doll. 'I bring her every Saturday. She's had quite a number of lessons already.'

'I beg your pardon,' said Teddy Robinson. 'Who are we talking about?'

'My little girl, Mary, of course,' said the doll, 'the one with the yellow curls.'

'Oh,' said Teddy Robinson, 'I thought we were talking about my little girl, Deborah, the one with the red ribbon.'

The doll didn't seem to hear. She was staring at the children with a fixed smile. Miss Silver was arranging them in two rows, the girls on one side, the boys on the other.

Teddy Robinson and the walkie-talkie doll both kept their eyes fixed on the girls' row.

'She looks so pretty, doesn't she?' said the doll. 'I do admire her dress, don't you?'

'Yes,' said Teddy Robinson, looking at Deborah.

'That pale blue suits her so well,' said the doll.

'Thank you,' said Teddy Robinson, 'I'm glad you like it; but it isn't pale blue – it's white.'

'Oh no, it's pale blue,' said the doll. 'I helped her mother to choose it myself.'

Teddy Robinson looked puzzled.

'Are you talking about the little girl with the red hair-ribbon?' he asked.

'No, of course not,' said the doll. 'Why should I be? I'm talking about Mary.'

14

'Whoever is Mary?' said Teddy Robinson.

'The little girl we have all come to watch,' said the doll. '*My* little girl. We've been talking about her all the time.'

'*I* haven't,' said Teddy Robinson. 'I've been talking about Deborah.'

'Deborah?' said the doll. 'Whoever is Deborah?'

'What a silly creature this doll is!' said Teddy Robinson to himself. 'She doesn't seem able to keep her mind on the class at all.' And he decided not to bother about talking to her any more. Instead he listened to Miss Silver, who was teaching the boys and girls how to bow and curtsy to each other.

'I must watch this carefully,' said Teddy Robinson to himself. 'I should like to know how to bow properly – it might come in handy at any time. I might be asked to tea at Buckingham Palace or happen to meet the Queen out shopping one day, and I should look very silly if I didn't know how to make my bow properly.'

As the boys all bowed from the waist Teddy Robinson leaned forward on his chair.

'Lower!' cried Miss Silver.

The boys all bowed lower, and Teddy Robinson leaned forward as far as he could; but he went just a little too far, and a moment later he fell head over heels on to the floor. Luckily, no one knew he had been practising his bow, they just thought he had toppled off his chair by mistake, as anyone might – so they took no notice of him.

Then it was the girls' turn to curtsy. The line of

little girls wobbled and wavered, and Deborah wobbled so much that she too fell on the floor. But after three tries she did manage to curtsy without falling over, and Teddy Robinson was very proud of her.

'Never mind,' said Miss Silver, as she said good-bye to them at the end of the class. 'You did very well for a first time. You can't expect to learn to dance in one lesson. But you did enjoy it, didn't you?'

'Oh, yes!' said Deborah. 'It was lovely.'

'What did she mean?' said Teddy Robinson, as soon as they were outside. 'I thought you danced better than anybody.'

'Oh, no,' said Deborah. 'I think I was doing it all wrong, but it *was* fun. I'm glad we're going again next Saturday.'

'Well I never!' said Teddy Robinson. 'I quite thought you were the only one doing it right. Never mind. Did you see when I fell off the chair? That was me trying to bow. I don't think I did it very well either.'

'You did very well for a first time too,' said Deborah. 'You can't expect to learn to bow in one lesson. We must practise together at home, though. You can learn to bow to me while I practise doing my curtsy.'

'That will be very nice,' said Teddy Robinson. 'Then next time we shan't both end up on the floor.'

That night Teddy Robinson had a most Beautiful Dream. He dreamt he was in a very large theatre, with red velvet curtains, tied with large golden tassels, on each side of the stage.

"She belongs to that handsome bear in the front row."

Every seat in the theatre was full; Teddy Robinson himself was sitting in the middle of the front row, and all the people were watching Deborah, who was dancing all alone on the stage in her new pink dancing-shoes. She was dressed like a princess, in a frilly white dress with a red sash, and she had a silver crown on her head.

The orchestra was playing sweetly, and Deborah was dancing so beautifully that soon everyone was whispering and asking who she was.

Teddy Robinson heard someone behind him saying, 'She belongs to that handsome bear in the front row, the one in the velvet suit and lace collar.'

He felt himself floating through the air

Teddy Robinson looked round, but couldn't see any bear in a velvet suit and lace collar. The he looked down and saw that instead of his ordinary trousers he was wearing a suit of beautiful blue velvet, with a large lace collar fastened at the neck with a silver pin. And in his lap was a bunch of roses tied with silver ribbon.

'Goodness gracious, they must have meant me!' he thought, and felt his fur tingling with pleasure and excitement.

As the music finished and Deborah came to the front of the stage to curtsy, Teddy Robinson felt himself floating through the air with his bunch of roses, and a moment later he landed lightly on the stage beside her. A murmur went up from the audience, 'Ah, here is Teddy Robinson himself!'

bowed and curtsyed together

Folding one paw neatly across his tummy, he bowed low to Deborah. Then, as she took the roses from him and they both bowed and curtsyed again, everyone in the theatre clapped so loudly that Teddy Robinson woke up and found he was in bed beside Deborah.

At first he was so surprised that he could hardly believe he was really at home in bed, but just then Deborah woke up too. She rolled over, smiling, with her eyes shut, and said, 'Oh, Teddy Robinson, I've just had such a Beautiful Dream! I must tell you all about it.'

So she did. And the funny thing was that Deborah

had dreamt exactly the same dream as Teddy Robinson. She remembered every bit of it.

And that is the end of the story about how Teddy Robinson went to the dancing-class.

2

Teddy Robinson in Disguise

ONE day Teddy Robinson was sitting by a garden pool looking at the water-lilies when a toad suddenly slipped out of the water and scrambled up the bank. He sat by the edge of the pool and looked up at Teddy Robinson with tiny, bright eyes that shone like jewels.

'Hallo,' said Teddy Robinson, 'who are you?'

'I am a prince in disguise,' croaked the toad.

'What does that mean?' said Teddy Robinson.

'It means I look like a toad, but I'm really a prince.'

'Is that true?' asked Teddy Robinson.

'I hope so,' said the toad. 'It's the story I've always told.'

'It's a very nice story,' said Teddy Robinson. 'I wish I could think of one like that.'

'And who are you?' asked the toad.

Teddy Robinson thought quickly.

'I am a horse in disguise,' he said.

'You don't look like one,' said the toad.

'Nor do you look like a prince,' said Teddy Robinson.

'I never talk to rude people,' said the toad, and dived into the pool again.

Teddy Robinson had not meant to be rude and thought it rather silly of the toad to be so touchy, but he didn't mind. He went on staring at the water-lilies and thinking about what the toad had told him. He

"I am a prince in disguise"

decided it would be rather jolly to be someone in disguise.

Later on, when he was at home again, Teddy Robinson practised standing on four legs on the toy-cupboard.

'Whatever are you doing?' said Deborah.

'Who do you think I am?' said Teddy Robinson.

'You're my funny old bear standing on four legs. Why?'

'Oh,' said Teddy Robinson. 'I was rather hoping you would think I was the milkman's horse.'

'But why should I?' said Deborah. 'You don't *look* like a horse.'

A little later Teddy Robinson called to Deborah again. This time he was lying on his tummy with his paws stretched out in front of him.

"Who do you think I am?"

'Who am I now?' he asked. 'You can see I'm swimming.'

'A bear at the seaside?' said Deborah.

'No. A fish,' said Teddy Robinson crossly. 'You don't seem to know a disguise when you see one.'

'But I don't see one,' said Deborah. 'You have to *look* like someone if you're in disguise. It's no good just acting like someone. I'll show you one day, but not now. Andrew is coming and he's bringing Spotty, his toy dog.'

Teddy Robinson growled. '*Must* they come? I don't like Spotty. He argues too much. Can't we be out?'

'No. I've said we'll be in,' said Deborah. 'Andrew thought Spotty would be nice company for you.'

'I don't want company,' said Teddy Robinson. 'I want to be alone.'

'I didn't know you'd mind, or I wouldn't have asked

23

them,' said Deborah. 'But we can't stop them now, can we?'

Teddy Robinson began thinking hard. 'Tell them we've moved,' he said. 'Let's move house before they come.'

'That would be too difficult,' said Deborah.

'Let's move ourselves then,' said Teddy Robinson. 'Let's go away.'

'We can't. I said we'd be here.'

'Then let's think of some way to make them go past the house,' said Teddy Robinson. 'I know! Let's chalk arrows on the pavement going right on up the road.'

'But where would the arrows go to?' said Deborah.

They both thought hard about this. Then Teddy Robinson said, 'I know! Let the arrows go down the little hill into the pond. They'd be sure to follow them. People always follow arrows.'

'They'd get very wet,' said Deborah.

'We could write STOP HERE just by the railing,' said Teddy Robinson.

'Yes, that's true,' said Deborah.

'And we could leave them a little stool to sit on, and a book to read,' said Teddy Robinson kindly. 'Then they could stay there till it was time for them to go home again.'

'So they could,' said Deborah.

'Quick, get the chalk!' said Teddy Robinson.

So Deborah found the chalk and her little stool and a picture book, and put them all together in a paper carrier bag.

But at that moment the door-bell rang.

'Goodness, we're too late!' said Deborah. 'Here they are!'

'Hide me,' said Teddy Robinson. 'Oh, how I wish I were in disguise!'

Deborah emptied the things out of the paper bag.

'Here you are,' she said. 'This will do for a disguise.' She quickly poked two holes in the bag for him to see through, and slipped it over his head. 'Thank goodness it's paper,' she added, 'or you might suffocate.'

'But who am I meant to be?' said Teddy Robinson.

Deborah read the printing on the bag.

'It says: "Smith and Son, High-class Groceries, Family Business",' she said. 'You'd better be that.'

She slipped her Wellington boots over his feet. 'Now you are quite covered up,' she said. And at that moment the door opened and Andrew and Spotty came in.

'Didn't you hear the door-bell?' asked Andrew. 'Your mummy let us in. I was afraid you weren't here.'

'Teddy Robinson isn't,' said a deep, growly voice from under the paper bag.

'Where is he, then?' said Spotty.

Deborah said, 'I'm afraid you won't see him today. He's gone into business.'

'I don't know what that means exactly,' said Andrew.

'Nor do I,' said Deborah, 'but that's where Teddy Robinson's gone.'

'Who's that, then?' said Spotty, staring at the bag.

'That's Smith and Son,' said Deborah.

'I don't believe it,' said Spotty.

'All right, then – read it and see,' said the deep growly voice from under the bag.

'I can't – it's upside down,' said Spotty.

'Huh! Some people can't even read things upside down!' said the growly voice.

'And *some* people can't even read things the right way up,' said Spotty. 'Teddy Robinson can't for one.'

Teddy Robinson nearly shouted, 'I can! – short words, anyway,' but he remembered just in time and said, 'I'm Mr Smith and Son, High-class Groceries – that's who I am.'

'I don't believe it,' said Spotty again.

Andrew lifted him on to the stool beside Teddy Robinson, and Spotty peered over the top of the paper bag to spell out the writing.

'Smith and Son – so it is!' he said. 'But I still don't believe it.'

'Don't believe what?' said Deborah.

'What it says on the bag,' said Spotty.

'Well, it's silly to argue all day,' said Deborah. 'Let's go out for a walk.'

So Deborah, Andrew, and Spotty all went out, and Teddy Robinson stayed sitting on the cupboard under the bag.

It was dark inside, and it smelt of bacon and coffee and all sorts of nice things mixed together.

Teddy Robinson began singing a little song about it:

'I like coffee,
I like tea,
I like bacon in with me.

26

"Smith and Son – so it is! But I still don't believe it"

I like biscuit,
I like bun,
I like being Smith and Son.'

In a minute the door opened, and Teddy Robinson
heard someone come into the room and start opening
drawers and cupboards. A moment later the bag was
lifted off his head, and there was Mummy smiling at
him with her arms full of clothes.

'Whatever are you doing there?' she said, laughing;
and, tucking him under her arm, she carried him into
the kitchen with the paper bag and the bundle of
clothes.

'Here we are,' said Mummy, putting them all down
on the table. 'I've found quite a lot of things that are

too small for Deborah now. I shall be glad if you can use them for Marlene, and here is a bag to put them in.'

Teddy Robinson looked round and saw that Mummy was talking to Mrs White, who sometimes came to help with the cleaning. She was sitting at the table with her little girl, Marlene, on her lap.

Mummy and Mrs White began sorting out the clothes and holding them up against Marlene to see if they fitted.

'Oh, here is one of Debbie's first baby dresses!' said Mummy, 'and the little bonnet that went with it. These are too small even for Marlene. I should think they would just fit Teddy Robinson.'

She put the dress on him, tied the bonnet under his chin, and wrapped him in an old baby-shawl. Then she held him out to Marlene.

'There you are,' she said, 'there's a baby for you.'

'Oh, dear!' thought Teddy Robinson, 'I hope I'm not being given away.'

But Mummy said, 'Not to keep; only to play with while we're talking. We couldn't give Teddy Robinson away.'

Marlene hugged him tightly and toddled out of the back door. Her own push-chair was waiting outside. She sat Teddy Robinson in it, then pushed him along to the garden, and there she wheeled him happily round and round the lawn.

Teddy Robinson was happy too. It was great fun to

be disguised as a very small baby when he was really a middling-sized, middle-aged bear. He began singing:

> 'Round and round the garden
>   like a teddy bear –'

then he suddenly remembered he wasn't like a teddy bear at all – he was like a baby, so he changed it to:

> 'Round and round the garden
>   in the open air,
>   looking like a baby,
>   *not* a teddy bear . . .'

When Mummy called Marlene in to have some tea Teddy Robinson stayed sitting in the push-chair in the garden. Soon he heard voices and guessed that Deborah, Andrew, and Spotty were coming back from their walk. He couldn't see, because he had his back to the house, but it sounded as if Spotty was still arguing.

'– it depends what you mean by *high-class* groceries,' he was saying. 'How do we know they were? You can't believe everything you see written on a paper bag.'

'Oh, Spotty, do stop!' said Deborah in a tired voice. 'You've talked about nothing else the whole afternoon.'

Teddy Robinson laughed to himself under the baby's bonnet.

'I always said he argued too much,' he said to himself and was glad to think he had missed the walk with Spotty.

The front gate banged, and he heard foorsteps coming down the side path towards the back door. Suddenly

...laughed to himself under the baby's bonnet

they stopped, and he heard Deborah's voice say, 'Hallo! There's a strange baby in our garden. We must have got visitors.'

'Bother,' said Andrew. 'I suppose we'd better go, then.'

'I hate babies,' said Spotty.

'I rather like them,' said Deborah. 'Wait here a minute and I'll see who it is.'

She ran up to the push-chair, and Teddy Robinson nearly laughed out loud when he saw her surprised face.

'It's *you*!' she said. 'I thought you were a real baby!'

'Hush!' said Teddy Robinson. 'Don't tell them it's me. Have they gone yet?'

Deborah looked round. 'Not yet,' she said.

'I'll soon make them go,' said Teddy Robinson, and he began making a noise like a baby crying – a cross, tired, whining baby.

'That's why I hate babies,' said Spotty to Andrew. 'They're boring. Let's go.'

Deborah looked round again.

'Yes, this *is* rather a boring baby,' she said. 'It looks as if it's going to go on crying for a long while, too. Perhaps you had better go home.'

'All right. Good-bye,' said Andrew.

Just then Spotty caught sight of the paper bag that Mrs White had put out on the back step, ready to take home.

'*There* you are!' he said "Smith and Son, High-class Groceries". And they're not high-class groceries at all; they're old clothes! I *said* you couldn't believe what you saw written on a bag. I *said* it all depended what you meant by . . .'

Andrew carried him away still arguing.

Deborah laughed and hugged Teddy Robinson.

'That *was* a good disguise!' she said. 'However did you do it?'

'Oh, it was quite easy,' said Teddy Robinson. 'I'm getting rather good at disguises now, aren't I? Do you remember ages ago, when I was quite a young bear, how I thought I could look like a horse by just standing on four legs?'

'Yes,' said Deborah. 'But that wasn't ages ago – that was only this afternoon.'

'Was it really?' said Teddy Robinson. 'Well, it seems ages ago to me. I've had quite a lot of fun since then.'

And that is the end of the story about Teddy Robinson in disguise.

3

Teddy Robinson Stops Growing

ONE day Teddy Robinson was watching Deborah digging in her garden. There was a nice fresh smell in the air, the sun shone warm on his fur, and he thought how nice it was to be out of doors again after the long, cold winter.

Soon he heard a rustling noise near by and saw that a large pile of leaves was moving. A moment later the garden tortoise poked his head out and looked round, blinking.

'Hallo,' said Teddy Robinson. 'Where have you been?'

'Merry Christmas,' said the tortoise.

'Thank you,' said Teddy Robinson, 'but Christmas was over long ago.'

'Happy New Year, then,' said the tortoise.

'Thank you again,' said Teddy Robinson, 'but it isn't New Year either. I rather think this is spring.'

'Ah, better still!' said the tortoise. 'I always come up in spring. I went down under ground last autumn when the leaves fell off the trees – felt I couldn't stand the cold winter, you know.'

'Oh, dear, then, I'm afraid you did miss Christmas!' said Teddy Robinson. 'What a pity!'

'Never mind,' said the tortoise, 'we can't all have

33

everything. You had your Christmas and I had my nice warm bed. Tell me, what's new? How is the old place?' He peered round the garden, blinking in the sunlight.

'My word!' he said, 'that hedge has grown thick.'

'Has it?' said Teddy Robinson. 'I never noticed.'

'Oh, yes,' said the tortoise; 'last year it hardly – I say! Who is that very large person digging over there?'

'That's not a large person,' said Teddy Robinson. 'That's Deborah. Does she know you're out yet?'

'Deborah?' said the tortoise. 'Goodness me! I must go and see her.' And he waddled off down the path.

Mummy came out into the garden.

'Oh, look! Dear old Tortle is back,' she said. 'Spring is really here. How good it is to see everything growing, and Tortle coming out again, and the days growing longer!'

She found a cabbage-leaf for Tortle, and Deborah filled a little dish with water for him to drink.

'That reminds me,' said Mummy, 'your daffodil needs watering, and so does Teddy Robinson's. Run and get them.'

Deborah and Teddy Robinson each had a daffodil in a flowerpot. Auntie Sue had brought them at Christmas. For a long while Teddy Robinson had watched his carefully every day to see if he could see it growing, but lately he had forgotten all about it.

Deborah brought the pots out into the garden.

'Just look how tall they are!' she said. 'Last time we looked they weren't nearly as big.'

'Now, how did they do that?' said Teddy Robinson.

"Now, how did they do that?"

'Well, we watered them sometimes,' said Deborah. 'I think that helped. And when they were new we put them in the dark in the cupboard, do you remember? Auntie Sue said that was the way to start them growing.'

'And Auntie Sue is coming to tea today,' said Mummy. 'I must get back to my baking.'

Deborah carried the daffodils back into the house, and Teddy Robinson sat in the sun and sang to himself because it was spring and everything was so jolly.

In a minute the puppy from over the road came galloping up. He was so pleased to see Teddy Robinson that he bowled him over like a ball, then ran round him in circles.

'Hallo, little teddy bear,' he said. 'Sorry if I upset you. How do you like my new collar?'

Teddy Robinson tried to look as if he had been rolling in the grass on purpose.

'I'm not a little teddy bear,' he said, 'I'm a good middling-sized bear. But let's see your new collar.'

The puppy stood still, and Teddy Robinson saw that he was wearing a big brown collar with gold studs all round it.

'That is very fine,' he said, 'but what's happened to the little red one you used to wear?'

'Grown out of it!' said the puppy proudly. 'This is my first grown-up collar. They say I'm growing fast. Isn't it fun! You're not growing much, are you?'

'Perhaps not at the moment,' said Teddy Robinson. 'I've too much else to think about. I expect I shall soon, though.'

'I wonder you don't start now,' said the puppy. 'Where is everybody?'

'Indoors,' said Teddy Robinson. 'Mummy's baking.'

'Oh, is she?' said the puppy. 'That's interesting.' And he wandered off towards the house, sniffing the air.

Teddy Robinson lay in the long grass and thought hard.

'Everything seems to be growing,' he said to himself. 'The hedge is growing thicker, the days are growing longer, the daffodils are growing taller, and now even that pup says he's growing bigger. Well, I only hope I'm growing too.'

'But you're not, you know,' said Tortle. 'Last year I

could reach the top of your foot with my nose, and this year I find I still can.'

'Dear me!' said Teddy Robinson. 'Oh, dearie me!'

'Don't worry,' said the tortoise. 'Life is sweet. Spring is here, and time goes on and on, and round and round. Life is very sweet, teddy bear; why should you bother about growing?'

'I wouldn't, only everyone else seems to,' said Teddy Robinson.

When Deborah came out again he said, 'What would happen if you put me in a flowerpot and watered me?'

'You'd get very wet,' said Deborah.

'Is that all? Wouldn't anything else happen?'

'No. What else could happen?' said Deborah. She had forgotten about the daffodils now and thought it was a very silly-bear question.

After a while Teddy Robinson said, 'You know, I've started thinking about cupboards now.'

'Have you?' said Deborah. 'What sort of cupboards?'

'Dark cupboards,' said Teddy Robinson.

'How many of them?' said Deborah.

'One would do,' said Tebby Robinson.

'What for?' said Deborah.

'For me to sit in,' said Teddy Robinson.

'What *do* you mean?' said Deborah.

'I was only thinking how much I should like to sit in a dark cupboard for a little while,' said Teddy Robinson.

'What a funny old boy you are!' said Deborah. 'I suppose you can sit in a dark cupboard if you want to. But I won't sit with you. I don't like dark cupboards.'

'Oh, I do!' said Teddy Robinson. 'Can I sit in one now?'

'Yes, I suppose so, if you really mean it,' said Deborah. So she carried him indoors and put him in the cupboard under the stairs on top of a pile of old newspapers.

'Is that what you really want?' she asked.

'Yes, thank you,' said Teddy Robinson. 'Good-bye.'

'Good-bye,' said Deborah. 'When shall I fetch you?'

'I really ought to stay here about six weeks,' said Teddy Robinson, 'but dinner-time will do.'

So Deborah shut the door, and Teddy Robinson sat quite still in the dark and waited to begin growing. The daffodils had been no bigger than bulbs when they were first put in the cupboard, and now they were as tall as he was.

'So there's no knowing *how* big I may grow,' said Teddy Robinson to himself, 'because I was quite a good middling-sized bear when I came in.'

To help himself start growing he began singing about all the biggest things he could think of:

'Elephants,
and giants,
and hippopotami,
tall giraffes
with heads so high
they nearly reach the sky . . .'

and soon he felt a sort of tingling in his fur.

'Hooray,' he thought, 'I'm sure I'm beginning to

38

grow.' His arms began to feel like large furry sausages, and his legs began to feel like huge furry tree-trunks.

'Yes,' he said, 'I'm sure I'm growing bigger and bigger. I wonder how long it will be before my head touches the ceiling. Perhaps I shall grow too big for the cupboard and burst right out of it.'

He began singing again, in a big, booming voice:

> 'Elephants,
> and giants,
> and hippopotami
> can never be
> as big as me
> or half as tall as I.'

And then at last Deborah came, and Teddy Robinson was brought out into the daylight again. But she didn't say, 'Oh, Teddy Robinson, how big you've grown!' All she said was, 'I'm, sure you don't want to sit in this dusty old cupboard any more. Let's go out in the garden.'

Teddy Robinson was surprised.

'Don't I look any different?' he asked as they went out.

'Yes,' said Deborah, 'you've got a cobweb on your head. Oh – and there's a spider running about in your fur!'

She shook it out on to the grass.

'Is that all?' said Teddy Robinson.

'Yes,' said Deborah, wiping away the cobweb. 'Now you look just as usual.' And she kissed him on the nose.

Teddy Robinson was disappointed not to have grown big enough to surprise everybody, but he still thought he must have grown a *little* bit; so after a while he said, 'Do you remember when you used to stand me up against the wall to see how tall I was?'

'Yes,' said Deborah.

'My nose used to come just above your knee, didn't it?'

'I believe it did,' said Deborah.

'Well,' said Teddy Robinson, 'I think perhaps it may come a *little* higher now. Shall we try and see?'

So Deborah stood him up against the wall.

Teddy Robinson stared at Deborah's legs, but his nose came quite a bit *lower* than her knees!

'Are you standing on tiptoe?' he asked.

'No,' said Deborah. 'Truly I'm not.'

'And are you sure I'm standing, not sitting?'

'Quite sure,' said Deborah, stepping backwards to look.

'Well I never!' said Teddy Robinson, and he was so surprised he fell flat on his face.

Deborah stood him up against the wall again.

'How high do you come up?' she said. 'Let's see.'

'*Below* your knees,' said Teddy Robinson. 'Just look!'

'So you do!' said Deborah. 'How funny I never noticed! It almost seems as if you're growing *smaller*, doesn't it?'

'That's just what I was thinking,' said Teddy Robinson sadly. 'I'm afraid you're right.'

"How high do you come up?"

When Deborah was called in to change her dress and have her hair brushed Teddy Robinson stayed under the apple-tree. He didn't feel like having his fur brushed for Auntie Sue, and, anyway, he was afraid his best purple dress wouldn't fit him any more now that he was growing so small.

'I wish I'd never sat in that silly cupboard,' he said. 'How was I to know it would make me grow smaller?'

He began singing to himself in a small, sad voice:

> 'The days are growing longer,
>   the grass is growing high,

it seems to me
the apple-tree
can nearly reach the sky.

The plants are growing bigger,
and Debbie's growing tall;
how sad to be
a bear like me
who's only growing small.'

There was a sudden snuffling and scuffling, and the puppy from over the road came bounding across the grass, carrying something rather large in his mouth.

'What have you got there?' said Teddy Robinson.

The puppy dropped what he was carrying on to the flower bed. Then he looked quickly over his shoulder, licked his lips, and said, 'Chocolate cake. Like a piece?'

'No, thank you. Where did you get it from?'

'Off your kitchen table,' said the puppy. 'It *is* fun – I find I can just reach it if I stand on my back legs! I never used to be able to. Can you?'

'No,' said Teddy Robinson.

'You know what?' said the puppy, gobbling cake, 'I think I'm growing bigger and you're growing smaller.'

'I know,' said Teddy Robinson, 'but don't let's talk about it. That cake was for tea. Are you going to eat it all?'

'I thought I'd eat half and bury the rest,' said the puppy. 'It might come in handy later.'

Teddy Robinson watched while the puppy scrabbled in the earth and buried the other half of the cake.

"Chocolate cake. Like a piece?"

'It might grow if you leave it long enough,' he said. 'A chocolate-cake-tree would be nice, wouldn't it?'

A motor-car horn hooted loudly at the front gate.

'That will be Auntie Sue,' said Teddy Robinson.

The puppy dived under the hedge out of sight, and a moment later Auntie Sue and Deborah came into the garden.

'How big you're growing, Debbie!' said Auntie Sue. 'And how is dear Teddy Robinson? Oh, there he is, just the same as ever!' she said, as she caught sight of him sitting under the apple-tree.

'Well, anyway, she doesn't seem to notice that I'm growing smaller,' thought Teddy Robinson.

Mummy came out from the garden door.

43

'Does anyone know what's happened to my chocolate cake?' she called. 'I left it on the kitchen table and now it's gone. It's most peculiar. Where can it be?'

But, of course, nobody knew except Teddy Robinson, and he didn't say.

'Perhaps you forgot to make it,' said Deborah.

'But I'm sure I made it,' said Mummy. 'I remember putting it out to cool. And now there's nothing for tea.'

'Never mind,' said Auntie Sue. 'Let's all drive into town and buy some buns, then we can take our tea into the woods. It's a lovely day for a picnic.'

The puppy crawled out, wagging his tail.

'That will be fun!' he whispered to Teddy Robinson. 'I love a picnic. All the food is on the ground, and you can taste a bit of everything while people are talking.'

'Oh, here's Pup!' said Deborah. 'Can he come too?'

'Goodness, no!' said Auntie Sue. 'He's far too big for my little car. He has grown much bigger since I last saw him!'

'What about Teddy Robinson?' said Deborah. 'Can he come?'

'Yes, of course,' said Auntie Sue. 'There will always be enough room for Teddy Robinson.'

'I'm glad I'm not too big to fit into the car, anyway,' said Teddy Robinson, as Deborah quickly changed his trousers for his best purple dress, 'but I hope I shan't grow *very* much smaller.'

'Oh, I forgot to tell you!' said Deborah. 'It's all right about your growing smaller. I asked Mummy and she says you're not. It's only me growing bigger. Mummy

44

says people stop growing when they're big enough. She has.'

The puppy watched sadly as they all climbed into the car. Teddy Robinson felt quite sorry for him.

'Never mind, you've still got the cake,' he whispered.

'Why, so I have!' said the puppy. 'I'd forgotten all about it!' And he galloped off quite happily to dig it up again.

'I *am* glad I've stopped growing,' said Teddy Robinson to Deborah as they set off. 'If I'd grown any bigger I shouldn't have been able to come on the picnic; and if I'd grown any smaller I shouldn't be able to wear my best purple dress. As it is, I seem to be exactly right after all. I think I'll stay this size always.'

And that is the end of the story about how Teddy Robinson stopped growing.

4

Teddy Robinson is a Baby-Sitter

ONE day Teddy Robinson was dozing on top of the toy-cupboard when Deborah suddenly ran into the room and began tying a large white handkerchief round his tummy.

'Hallo!' said Teddy Robinson, waking up, 'what's this?'

Deborah fixed a smaller white handkerchief round his head and tied it in a knot behind.

'What am I going to be?' said Teddy Robinson. Deborah held him up to the looking-glass.

'What do you think you look like?' she asked.

'A nurse?' said Teddy Robinson. 'Yes, I do look rather like a nurse. Is that what I'm going to be?'

'Not exactly,' said Deborah, 'but something very like it, and a cap and apron suit you very well. You're going to be a baby-sitter.'

'*Am* I?' said Teddy Robinson. 'Tell me about it.'

So Deborah told him how Mrs Green had come, bringing her new baby with her in a pram, and, as it was time for the baby's rest, she and Mummy had decided to put him in the front garden while they talked together indoors.

'And I suddenly thought what a good baby-sitter you

46

"Yes, I do look rather like a nurse "

would make,' said Deborah, 'so I came to fetch you. Do you think you will like it?'

'Yes,' said Teddy Robinson, feeling rather pleased and proud, 'but I'm not quite sure what I have to do.'

'Just watch the baby, that's all,' said Deborah.

'That will be very nice,' said Teddy Robinson. 'I know how to watch toast, but I've never watched a baby before. Yes, I'll enjoy that. I'm rather good at watching things.'

Half-way down the stairs he suddenly said, 'I say! You don't think I'm too fat, do you?'

'How do you mean?' said Deborah.

'Too fat to sit on a baby, I mean,' said Teddy Robinson. 'I should like to be a baby-sitter very much, but I'd be sorry if I squashed the poor little thing.'

'Oh, no, that will be all right,' said Deborah. 'I don't think baby-sitters have to sit *on* the baby. It's good enough if they just sit *by* them.'

So they went out into the front garden, and there was Mrs Green's baby, fast asleep in his pram under the hawthorn-tree, looking very quiet and happy. Deborah lifted Teddy Robinson up so that he could see over the edge of the pram, and he made soft, teddy-bear noises at the baby.

'That's right,' said Deborah. 'I'm sure you'll be a very good baby-sitter.' And she sat him down in the other end of the pram, then ran indoors to talk to Mrs Green.

Teddy Robinson liked being a baby-sitter very much. It was pleasant and peaceful in the garden, the birds sang in the trees, and the breeze fluttered his handkerchief cap. He began singing to himself softly:

> 'Underneath the hawthorn-tree
> who should baby-sit but me?
> Wise and willing,
> neatly dressed,
> watching baby have his rest.
> Kind and cosy,
> here I am,
> baby-sitting in the pram.'

There was a fluttering overhead, and a moment later a sparrow flew down and perched on the edge of the pram.

'Hallo, who have we here?' he chirped, looking brightly at the baby with his head on one side.

'This is Mrs Green's baby,' said Teddy Robinson proudly, 'and I am the baby-sitter.'

'Really?' said the sparrow. 'Forgive my saying so, but I don't think you're sitting very well. My own babies have just hatched out nicely, but I don't think they would have if I hadn't sat on them a good deal better than that. How can you expect to keep him warm if you sit right at the other end of the nest?'

'Yes, but this baby isn't an egg,' said Teddy Robinson. 'I was told it was quite right to sit at this end.'

'Oh,' said the sparrow, 'perhaps you're right. He's a nice-looking baby, I must say.'

'Tell me,' said Teddy Robinson, '– you have babies of your own, so you should know – why has he no fur on his head? He's quite a new baby, I know, and I'm sure he was an expensive one; it seems a shame his fur should have worn off already, doesn't it?'

The sparrow looked at the baby carefully.

'I think it's all right,' he said. 'It's probably meant to be like that. My babies don't have feathers on when they're new, either.'

'It that so?' said Teddy Robinson. 'My own fur is a little thin on top, but I shouldn't have thought it was because I was new. Perhaps it's different for teddy bears.'

'I expect so,' said the sparrow. 'What a very nice nest you have here! My own nest is up in that tree. I almost think I should have preferred yours if I'd seen it first; that blanket looks so soft and warm. But, of course, a nest on wheels is rather a newfangled idea. I'm not sure that my wife would have liked it. Poor bird, she works very hard: I wish I could find someone as good as you to help her. I suppose you wouldn't like the job of baby-sitting for us sometime?'

Teddy Robinson was about to say thank you, but he was afraid he would be rather too big to sit in a bird's nest, when the sparrow suddenly flew up into the tree, and at the same moment the next-door kitten came padding softly along the garden wall.

'Hallo,' she said, 'what are you doing there?'

'I'm baby-sitting,' said Teddy Robinson.

'What a charming home you have for your baby,' said the kitten, admiring the pram. 'My mother has just had a new litter of kittens. I must tell her about this. It would be a delightful place for her to keep them in.'

Teddy Robinson was just going to say no, that wouldn't do at all because the pram already belonged to Mrs Green's baby, when the kitten suddenly scrambled up the tree, and at the same moment the puppy from over the road came lolloping up the path, wagging his tail.

'Hallo,' he said, 'what are you doing up there?'

'I'm baby-sitting,' said Teddy Robinson.

'Are you really? That's a jolly nice puppy-basket on wheels,' said the puppy from over the road, and he stood up on his hind legs, trying to see inside the pram.

'Please don't do that,' said Teddy Robinson. 'I'm afraid you'll wake the baby.'

Just then the puppy caught sight of the kitten half-way up the tree, and began barking loudly. The kitten scrambled higher up the tree and sat on a branch hissing and spitting, and the sparrows (who thought the kitten was after their babies at the top of the tree) began chirping and twittering and flapping their wings.

Teddy Robinson said, 'Hush!' and 'Please be quiet,' and '*Do* you mind not making so much noise?'; but no one took any notice of him. They went on barking, and hissing, and spitting, and cheeping, and twittering, and flapping, until at last he drew a deep breath and shouted at the top of his voice, 'GO AWAY, ALL OF YOU! I won't have you all quarrelling and shouting like this!'

Then the kitten scampered away, the puppy ran out of the gate, the sparrows stopped cheeping, and it was quiet again in the garden.

'I should think so too,' said Teddy Robinson to himself. 'I never heard such a noise. It was enough to wake anybody's baby.'

And, sure enough, at that moment the baby opened its eyes and mouth and began crying.

'Oh, dear,' said Teddy Robinson, 'please don't cry! I don't know what to do to make you stop, but it does make me look such a silly baby-sitter if I can't.'

But the baby went on crying.

After a while the sparrow flew down from the tree again. He perched on the edge of the pram and stared down into the baby's open mouth. Then he turned to Teddy Robinson.

'That baby's hungry,' chirped the sparrow. 'Look how wide open his beak is.'

'Do you really think so?' said Teddy Robinson.

51

"That baby's hungry"

A yellow-hammer from a near-by tree suddenly called out, 'A little bit of bread and no cheese!'

'No,' said the sparrow, 'what the baby needs is a nice little feed of worms. I'll go and see if I can find some.' And he flew off.

The next-door kitten came walking along the wall again.

'*Mia-ow-ow!*' she said, 'What a mewing! He's hungry.'

'Do you really think so?' said Teddy Robinson.

'Yes,' said the kitten, 'what that baby needs is a nice little bowl of fish. I'll go and see if I've got any left.' And she jumped down into the next-door garden.

The puppy from over the road came back.

'*Woof!*' he said. 'What a terrible whining and howling!'

'I know,' said Teddy Robinson, 'I think he's hungry.'

"What that baby needs is a nice little bowl of fish"

'Oh, no,' said the puppy, 'he's not hungry. He's probably teething. What that baby needs is a nice big juicy bone to help his teeth come through. I'll go and dig one up.' And he went galloping away over the road into his own garden.

And still the baby went on crying.

Teddy Robinson sat in the pram feeling very muddled and worried. Everyone had told him something different, and they all seemed perfectly sure they were right. Only Teddy Robinson didn't feel sure about anything at all. The baby was still crying, and he could hear the voices of the others from all around.

'A nice little feed of worms!' the sparrow was chirping from the garden bed.

'A nice little bowl of fish!' the kitten was mewing from the next-door garden.

53

'A nice big juicy bone!' the puppy was barking from over the road.

And, 'A little bit of bread and no cheese!' called the yellow-hammer over and over again.

'Oh, dear!' said Teddy Robinson, 'I wonder which of them is right. Or are they all right? I wish I knew.'

An old lady came walking slowly up the road. She stopped at the gate when she heard the baby crying.

'Dear, dear, poor little thing!' she said to herself. 'What that baby needs is a nice little lullaby – a soothing little song to send it to sleep. I'd stay and sing to it myself if I hadn't got to go home and get tea ready. Dear, dear, poor little thing!' And she went slowly on up the road, shaking her head.

'Why, of course!' said Teddy Robinson to himself. 'Why ever didn't I think of it before?' And he began singing to the baby in a gentle, soothing growl:

'Hush-a-bye,
hush-a-bye,
this is Teddy's lullaby.
Fold your paws
and close your eyes,
no more growling,
no more sighs;
shut your mouth
and please don't cry,
Teddy R. is sitting by
singing you a lullaby,
hush-a-bye,
hush-a-bye . . .'

54

and by the time he had got as far as this the baby was fast asleep.

'There now,' said Teddy Robinson, smiling to himself, 'I wonder why I listened to all those others. *I'm* the baby-sitter, not them. Of course I should know how to send a baby to sleep.'

And when Deborah came running out a moment later the garden was as quiet and peaceful as if the baby had never woken up at all.

'It's tea-time, Teddy Robinson,' said Deborah. 'Would you like to come in now?'

'Oh, yes,' said Teddy Robinson, 'that would be very nice. Baby-sitting is harder work than I thought. I shall be quite glad to sit down and have a rest.'

And that is the end of the story about how Teddy Robinson was a baby-sitter.

5

Teddy Robinson is Brave

ONE day Teddy Robinson woke up in the morning feeling very brave and jolly. Even before Deborah was awake he began singing a little song, telling himself all about how brave he was. It went like this:

> 'Jolly brave me,
> jolly brave me,
> the bravest bear
> you ever did see;
>
> as brave as a lion
> or tiger could be,
> as brave as a dragon –
> oh, jolly brave me!'

And by the time Deborah woke up he was beginning to think he was quite the bravest bear in the whole world.

'Whatever is all this shouting and puffing and blowing?' asked Deborah, opening her eyes sleepily.

'Me fighting a dragon,' said Teddy Robinson, puffing out his chest:

> 'Bang, bang, bang, you're dead,
> sang the Brave Bear on the bed.
> The dragon trembled, sobbed, and sighed,
> "Oh, save my life!" he cried . . . and died.'

"Bang, bang, bang, you're dead"

'You see? I killed him!' said Teddy Robinson.

'But I don't see any dragon,' said Deborah.

'No, he's gone now,' said Teddy Robinson. 'Shall we get up? It's quite safe.'

Half-way through the morning the phone-bell rang. Mummy was busy, so Deborah lifted the receiver, but before she had time to say 'hallo' Teddy Robinson said, 'I'll take it! It may be someone ringing up to ask me to fight a dragon.' And he said 'Hallo,' in a deep, brave growl.

'Hallo,' said Daddy's voice, 'that's Teddy Robinson, isn't it? How are you?'

'I'm better, thank you,' said Teddy Robinson.

'Oh, I didn't know you'd been ill,' said Daddy.

'I haven't,' said Teddy Robinson.

'Then how can you be better?' said Daddy.

'I'm not better than ill,' said Teddy Robinson. 'I'm better than better.'

'I see,' said Daddy. 'Now, will you tell Mummy I shall be back early today? And listen, I have a plan—'

'This isn't really me talking,' said Teddy Robinson. 'It's Deborah. Did you know?'

'I guessed it might be,' said Daddy. 'But it's you I want to talk to. How would you like to meet me for tea at Black's farm – and bring Deborah too, of course?'

'Will there be a dragon there?' asked Teddy Robinson.

'A what?' said Daddy.

Deborah pushed Teddy Robinson's nose away from the phone and talked to Daddy herself. 'Oh, yes!' she said. 'It would be lovely. Hold on and I'll fetch Mummy.'

When Mummy had finished talking to Daddy and deciding where they should meet she said, 'Won't that be nice? It's a long while since we had a walk in the country.'

'Will you like it, Teddy Robinson?' asked Deborah.

'I'm just wondering,' said Teddy Robinson. 'A walk in the country seems rather a soppy way for a Big Brave Bear to spend the afternoon.'

'Nonsense,' said Deborah. 'Daddy is much bigger and braver than you, and he doesn't think so. Shall I ask Andrew to come with us?'

'Not if he brings Spotty,' said Teddy Robinson.

'No,' said Deborah, 'we'll ask him to bring someone else instead.'

Andrew said he would like to come, and he would bring his clockwork mouse, who was small and easy to carry.

'A walk in the country will do her good,' said Andrew. 'She had rather a fright yesterday with a cat who thought she was real and chased her under the sofa.'

So after dinner they all set off.

Deborah and Andrew were excited to be going into the country. Teddy Robinson was still feeling very jolly and big and brave, but Mouse was a little trembly. She had really had quite a fright with the cat the day before.

'Are you sure we shan't run into danger?' she kept asking.

'Don't you worry,' said Teddy Robinson. 'I'm quite brave enough for two of us and I'll look after you. There's no need to worry while you're with me.'

'Thank you,' said Mouse. 'I'm sure I shall be quite safe with such a big, brave bear as you. I was only thinking – suppose it should thunder?'

'Well, what if it did?' said Teddy Robinson. '*I* shouldn't mind. I love thunder.'

'Or what if we should meet some cows?' said Mouse.

'Well, what if we did?' said Teddy Robinson. '*I* aren't frightened of cows. I should just walk bravely past and stare at them fiercely.' He began singing:

> 'Three cheers for me,
> for jolly brave me.
> Oh, what a jolly brave bear I be!'

Mouse said, 'Hip, hip, hooray,' three times over in a high, quavering voice. Then she said, 'Oh, yes – certainly, and I know now how brave you are. A fly settled on your nose while you were singing, and you never even blinked.'

'Pooh! That's nothing,' said Teddy Robinson. 'I killed a dragon before breakfast.'

'Whatever is Teddy Robinson talking about?' said Andrew to Deborah. 'What's the matter with him today?'

'I really don't know,' said Deborah. 'He woke up like it. I'm afraid he's showing off.'

When they got out into the open country Mouse and Teddy Robinson were put into Mummy's basket so that Andrew and Deborah could run about freely. They had a lovely time.

But soon a large black cloud came up, and there was a low rumbling noise in the distance.

'Oo-err,' said Mouse, 'I'm sure that's thunder. Are you frightened of thunder, Teddy Robinson?'

'What, me? I should hope not!' said Teddy Robinson. (There was another low rumble.) 'No – I hope not. Yes – I very much hope not.'

Deborah and Andrew came running up, saying, 'Look at that big black cloud!'

'Yes,' said Mummy. 'I don't much like the look of it.'

'Deborah,' said Teddy Robinson, 'are you frightened of thunder?'

'Mummy,' said Deborah, 'are you?'

'No,' said Mummy, 'but I think we ought to get under cover as soon as possible.'

Deborah turned to Teddy Robinson, 'Not much,' she said, 'but we ought to get under cover as soon as possible.'

Teddy Robinson turned to Mouse, 'No, *I* aren't frightened of thunder,' he said, 'but I've decided we ought to get under cover as soon as possible.'

Then they all began to run.

It wasn't a very bad storm and it hardly rained at all, but Mummy thought they had better hurry.

'We will take a short cut through this field,' she said.

'Oo-err,' said Mouse, 'but there are cows in that field. Do you like cows, Teddy Robinson?'

'Oh, yes,' said Teddy Robinson, 'I think I like cows. I'll just find out. Deborah, do you like cows?'

'Mummy,' said Deborah, 'do you like cows?'

'Oh, yes,' said Mummy, 'of course I do. They are dear, gentle animals, and they give us milk. Don't you like them?'

'Oh, yes,' said Deborah, 'I like them too. Don't you, Teddy Robinson?'

'Oh, yes,' said Teddy Robinson, 'I like them very much. At least, I hope I do.'

He turned to Mouse. 'Of course I like cows,' he said. 'I'd forgotten for the minute how much I like them. They give us dear, gentle milk. Don't you like them?'

'Yes – I do if you do,' said Mouse.

'Oh, I *love* cows,' said Teddy Robinson.

'So do I,' said Deborah.

"I didn't see you staring at them fiercely"

'So do I,' said Mouse, in a high, trembly voice.

'But I think,' said Teddy Robinson, 'I think it would be kinder if we all went *round* the field instead of walking through it. We don't want to disturb the poor, dear cows, do we?'

'Oh, no, we don't want to disturb them,' said Deborah. 'Let's go round by the hedge, then we can look for blackberries. *Please*, Mummy, let's go round by the hedge!'

So they all hurried round the edge of the field (much too quickly to look for blackberries) until they came to the gate on the other side. The cows watched them pass.

'I didn't see you staring at them fiercely,' said

Mouse to Teddy Robinson, as they went through into the lane.

'How could I? There wasn't time, with everyone running so fast,' said Teddy Robinson.

They crossed the lane, and there on the far side of another field they saw Black's farm.

'Come along,' said Mummy, 'we'll climb over the gate and cut across this field. I expect Daddy will be waiting.'

Half-way across the field a cow that they hadn't seen rose from its knees and came walking towards them.

'Oo-err,' said Mouse, 'run!'

The cow began galloping.

'Oh, dear!' said Teddy Robinson. 'Why did you tell it to run?'

'It's all right,' said Mummy, 'there's nothing to be frightened of.'

But Deborah said, 'Run, Mummy!' And Andrew said, 'Yes, let's run!' And before they had time to think about it they were all running as fast as they could.

Mouse and Teddy Robinson bounced up and down inside the basket until they were quite out of breath, and then all of a sudden a dreadful thing happened. Teddy Robinson bounced so high that he never came down in the basket at all. He came down in the grass, and there were Mummy and Deborah and Andrew still running farther and farther away from him towards the gate on the other side of the field. And the cow was coming nearer and nearer, puffing and galloping and snorting through its nose.

"Eat me now and get it over"

Poor Teddy Robinson! He couldn't do anything but just lie there and wait for it. He had forgotten all about how to be brave.

'And to think it was only this morning I killed a dragon!' he said to himself. 'Or did I? Perhaps it was only a pretend dragon, after all. Yes, now I come to think of it, I'm sure it was only a pretend dragon. But this is a terribly real cow – I can feel its hooves shaking the ground. Oh, my goodness, here it comes!'

The cow came thundering up, then bent its head down and sniffed at Teddy Robinson.

'Please don't wait,' said Teddy Robinson. 'Eat me now and get it over.'

'Mm-m-merr!' said the cow. 'Must I?'

'Don't you want to?' said Teddy Robinson. 'I thought that was what you were coming for.'

'No,' said the cow, 'I was only coming to see who you were. Mm-m-merr! What a funny little cow you are. I never saw a cow like you before.'

'I'm not a little cow,' said Teddy Robinson. 'I'm a middling-sized teddy bear.'

'Why are you looking at me with your eyes crossed?' said the cow.

'I'm not. I'm staring at you fiercely.'

'Mm-m-merr,' said the cow. 'I shouldn't if I were you. The wind might change and they might get stuck.'

'Why don't you say Moo?' said Teddy Robinson.

'Because I'm a country cow. Only story-book cows say Moo, not real cows.'

'Fancy that!' said Teddy Robinson. 'And are you fierce?'

'Terribly fierce,' said the cow.

Teddy Robinson trembled all over again.

'Yes,' said the cow, 'I eat grass and lie in the sun and look at the buttercups . . .'

'I don't call that very fierce,' said Teddy Robinson.

'Well, I'm sorry,' said the cow, 'but that's all the fierce I know how to be. I told you I'm a country cow. I'm only used to a quiet life.'

'Well, thank goodness for that!' said Teddy Robinson. 'Now tell me about life in the country.'

'Mm-m-merr,' said the cow, 'it's very quiet, very quiet indeed. Listen to it.'

Teddy Robinson listened, and all he could hear was the sound of the grasses rustling in the breeze, and the cow breathing gently through its nose.

'Yes,' he said, 'it is very quiet, ve-ry qui-et, ve-ry . . .' and a moment later he was asleep.

It seemed hours later that Farmer Black found him in the field, and he was taken into the farmhouse. And there were Deborah and Daddy and Mummy and Andrew and Mouse, all waiting for him, and all terribly glad to see him again.

'Oh, dear Teddy Robinson!' cried Deborah, 'I *am* so glad you're not lost. And *what* a brave bear you are! I am sorry I said you were showing off.'

'Yes, he really is brave,' said Andrew to Daddy. 'We all ran away, and only Teddy Robinson was brave enough to face the cow all by himself.'

'And stare at him fiercely,' squeaked Mouse.

Then Daddy said Teddy Robinson ought to have a medal, and he made one out of a silver milk-bottle top, and Deborah pinned it on to his braces, and everyone said, 'Three cheers for Teddy Robinson, our Best Big Brave Brown Bear!'

And that is the end of the story about how Teddy Robinson was brave.

6

Teddy Robinson and the Mermaid

ONE hot summer day Teddy Robinson lay on the beach at the seaside. Deborah and Philip were bathing, but Teddy Robinson had said he would rather stay in the sun and get brown, so he lay listening to the waves lapping, and the seagulls mewing, and the children shouting to each other in the distance, until he felt quite dreamy and dozy. And then suddenly he heard a small voice quite close by calling softly:

> 'Come, furry one, and swim with me,
> come swim with me, far out to sea . . .'

'But I can't swim,' said Teddy Robinson, and then he looked round quickly to see who he was talking to. But there was no one there, only the children playing in the distance.

'That's funny,' he said to himself, '*someone* asked me to go swimming, and there isn't anyone.'

When the others came back he asked Deborah, 'Did you call me to come swimming with you just now?' But she only laughed and said, 'Of course not, silly old boy. You can't swim!'

'I know I can't,' said Teddy Robinson, 'but someone asked me, just the same.'

'You must have been dreaming,' said Deborah. Then

67

"Now you look quite like a mermaid."

she shook the water out of her hair (because she had been bathing without a cap) until it looked like long strings of seaweed.

'You look almost like a mermaid,' said Philip.

Deborah wrapped the towel round her legs and sat with her feet curled up under her.

'Now you look quite like a mermaid,' said Teddy Robinson. 'Shall I sing to you while you comb your hair?'

'If you like,' said Deborah. So Teddy Robinson sang:

> 'A mermaid saw a teddy bear
> lying by the sea.
> "Come swim with me, dear teddy bear,
> come swim with me," said she.
> "I'll give you strings of pearls to wear,
> and fish an' chips for tea."'

68

'Oh, no,' said Deborah, 'I'm sure mermaids don't eat chips, and I don't think they'd care for teddy bears either.'

'Mine would,' said Teddy Robinson.

Philip said, 'There aren't any such things, anyway. And a good thing too.'

'Why is it a good thing?'

'Because they sink ships and drown sailors,' said Philip. 'I don't believe in them.'

'Nor do I,' said Deborah.

Teddy Robinson didn't say anything. If Deborah didn't believe in mermaids then he didn't either, of course, but he was still wondering who it was who had called to him so softly.

After dinner that day they all three hurried down to the beach again. Deborah and Philip had been lent a really big shrimping net and could think of nothing but how many shrimps they were going to catch. Teddy Robinson went with them (to keep an eye on them, he said). Mummy was coming later with the tea basket.

The tide was still out and the shallow pools were full of shrimps. Deborah sat Teddy Robinson down by a little pool, leaning against a rock, then she ran off with Philip.

The sun was hot and the sea made a soft swishing noise. Teddy Robinson thought how lucky he was not to have to run about like the others, in the hot sunshine in his fur coat, and began singing a little song to himself:

'How nice to be
beside the sea
with only me
for company,
not running round or having fun,
or catching shrimps with anyone,
but dreamy-dozing in the sun
beside the sea.
How nice to be
alone with me
beside the sea.'

'It's nicer still at the very bottom of the sea,' said a little voice close by.

Teddy Robinson opened his eyes wide and there in the pool at his feet he saw a mermaid. She had long hair like golden seaweed, which hung down her shoulders and floated in the water, and a shining silver fish's tail, covered in shells.

Teddy Robinson thought he had never seen anything so pretty, and then he suddenly remembered that he didn't believe in mermaids.

'I don't think I'd better talk to you,' he said. 'I don't believe in you.'

The Mermaid laughed and shook her wet hair so that it splashed his fur.

'I don't believe in you either,' she said. 'I saw you this morning, dozing in the sun with your fat tummy and those funny little furry stumps, and I said to myself, "I just don't believe it. It can't be real."'

'That's absurd,' said Teddy Robinson. 'Of course

I'm real.' Then he stared hard out to sea trying to look as if he was bored. He hoped that if he pretended the Mermaid wasn't there she wouldn't be there. But when he looked out of the corner of his eye a moment later he saw that she was still laughing at him and he felt rather silly.

'Well,' he said, 'it doesn't seem to matter whether we believe in each other or not. We're both still here, aren't we? Was it you who asked me to come swimming?'

'Yes,' said the Mermaid. 'I felt sorry for you, all by yourself on the beach. And now I see they've left you again. Even if you aren't real they shouldn't do that to you, poor fish.'

'I'm not a fish, I'm a teddy bear,' said Teddy Robinson.

'Oh,' said the Mermaid, 'I thought you were some sort of furry fish, though I wondered about those funny little stumps.' She looked at his fat, furry legs. 'But you are handsome in spite of them,' she said.

'Thank you,' said Teddy Robinson. 'I think you are very pretty too.'

'It is a pity no one loves you,' said the Mermaid.

'Oh, but they do!' said Teddy Robinson.

'Not as much as I would,' said the Mermaid. 'If you were mine I would teach you to swim.' She flicked her tail and it shone silver in the pool. 'If you will come and be my bear you shall have a tail like mine. Yours could be decorated, too, with shells like this.' And she laid a big, curly shell on his lap. 'That is a singing shell. You can have it for a present.'

71

'Oh, thank you,' said Teddy Robinson. 'But I don't think I'd better come with you. I'm a dry-land animal really.'

'It is so beautiful under the sea,' said the Mermaid. 'I have a palace made of coral where we could live. We could play hide-and-seek in the seaweed forests, and you could wear pearls in your fur. There are millions of pearls at the bottom of the sea.'

Teddy Robinson was pleased that she liked him, but of course he knew he would never leave Deborah.

'All the same,' he thought, 'she *has* gone off shrimping without me, so if I did go with the Mermaid just for a little while she wouldn't really miss me.'

He thought how pretty he would look with a silver tail decorated with shells like the big, curly one in his lap, and he had a picture in his mind of how he and the Mermaid would float through the seaweed forests to her palace at the bottom of the sea. Then, when it was time to go home again, how excited Deborah would be to see him come flashing through the waves to the shore, with his paws full of pearls!

Then the Mermaid began singing:

'Come live with me and be my bear
and you shall comb my golden hair,
far away and under the sea,
come be my bear and live with me,'

and she sang so sweetly that Teddy Robinson forgot all about Deborah shrimping farther along the beach with Philip, and all about Mummy soon coming down with

he had a picture in his mind of how he and the mermaid would float through the seaweed forests

the tea basket. He didn't even notice that the little waves were creeping nearer and nearer up the beach because the tide had turned.

'Perhaps I'll come just for a little while,' he said. 'Are you sure it will be safe?'

'Quite safe with me,' said the Mermaid. 'There is only one thing to remember. Always beware of fishing nets, shrimping nets, any kind of nets.'

'Why?' said Teddy Robinson.

'They are dangerous,' said the Mermaid. 'You might

73

the awful thought of perhaps having to swim round and round in a goldfish bowl for the rest of his life

get caught in one. And you wouldn't like to find yourself in a goldfish bowl, would you?'

Teddy Robinson remembered seeing goldfish in a
bowl once at someone else's house. He shivered at the
awful thought of perhaps having to swim round and
round in a goldfish bowl for the rest of his life.

'So, remember,' said the Mermaid, 'beware of nets.'
She took hold of his paw gently, smiling at him.

'Come,' she said, 'we will catch this little wave that
is just coming in. We will float out on it together.'

Teddy Robinson felt the water suddenly lapping

round him, and a moment later he was lifted off the sand and found himself floating away.

'Don't be afraid,' said the Mermaid, 'lie on your back and look up at the sky. I will look after you. Hold on to my hair.' And she wound a strand of it round his arm. Then she began singing:

> 'Come live with me and be my bear
>   far away from anywhere,
>   far away and under the sea
>   come be my bear and live with me.'

It was very lovely floating dreamily on the water, listening to the little waves lapping round his ears, and soon Teddy Robinson, too, began singing:

> 'How sweet to be a Water Bear
>   and hold a mermaid by her hair,
>   to float away, as light as air,
>   with water, water everywhere.'

But as they floated and sang together, staring up at the blue sky and the little white clouds, Teddy Robinson stopped feeling as light as air. He began to feel heavy and drowsy instead. Soon he found that instead of singing he was blowing bubbles, and then he saw that the sky above him was blurred. This was because he was not floating on top of the water any more, but just under it. He grew heavier and heavier and drowsier and drowsier.

'But this floating business is really very easy,' he said to himself. 'It doesn't seem to matter whether I float on

75

top of the water or underneath it, it's equally pleasant either way.'

'This way,' called the Mermaid. Her voice was fainter now, and Teddy Robinson could only dimly see her long hair floating on the water, but he was happy to think he would soon be floating through the seaweed forests and seeing the palace where she lived.

I must remember to pick a lot of pearls on the way, he thought dreamily.

Then suddenly he heard the Mermaid calling, in a voice like a seagull's scream, 'Look out! Mind the net! Swim for your life!'

'It's no good screaming at me like that,' said Teddy Robinson. 'I can't swim yet, I can only float. And very pleasant it is too.'

Then, before he had time to realize what was happening, he felt a net closing round him, and he was being drawn back to the shore.

Too late he remembered what the Mermaid had said, 'Always beware of fishing nets, shrimping nets, any kind of nets.' But there was nothing he could do about it now – it was too late. Teddy Robinson gave himself up for lost and stopped thinking altogether.

He felt the net being drawn along the sand on to the beach, and then he was lifted out and laid down on something warm. His ears were still full of the sound of the sea, but he could hear people talking and everything seemed gold all round him.

'Please don't put me in a goldfish bowl just yet,' he said.

Then he heard Deborah's voice laughing in his ear, and he saw that he was lying on the warm, dry sand in the golden sunshine. Deborah wrapped him up in her bathing towel and hugged him until the water squeezed out of him.

'Oh, *dear* Teddy Robinson!' she said. 'I so nearly lost you. You were floating out to sea when Philip saw you, and we only just managed to catch you in the shrimping net.'

'Did you catch the Mermaid as well?' said Teddy Robinson.

'How could we?' said Deborah. 'There wasn't one.'

'There was, and you nearly did,' he said.

But Deborah didn't believe him. She laughed and said, 'Of course there wasn't a mermaid, but look, there's a whole string of seaweed, it was wrapped all round your arm, and there was this lovely big curly shell in the net. It's the kind you can hear the sea in.'

She put the shell close to Teddy Robinson's ear, and first he heard the sound of the sea, and then he thought he heard a far-away little voice singing:

> 'Come live with me and be my bear,
>   far away from anywhere,
>   far away and under the sea,
>   come be my bear and live with me . . .'

'Oh, no,' said Teddy Robinson, talking into the shell as if it were a telephone, 'if I'd come with you I should have drowned. And you're quite wrong about nets. It was the shrimping net that saved me.'

'Dear old, silly old, funny old bear,' said Deborah, 'whatever are you talking about?'

So Teddy Robinson told her. And by the time he had finished, the sun had nearly dried his fur again, Philip had caught a whole bucketful of shrimps, and Deborah did believe in mermaids after all.

And that is the end of the story about Teddy Robinson and the Mermaid.

7

Teddy Robinson and the Band

ONE day Teddy Robinson and Deborah and Mummy all went off to spend the afternoon in the park.

When they got there Mummy found a comfortable seat to sit on and settled down to knit. Deborah and Teddy Robinson sat down on the other end of the seat and looked around to see what they could see.

Not far away some children were skipping on the grass. After she had watched them for a little while Deborah said, 'I think I'd like to go and skip with those children, Teddy Robinson. You wouldn't mind staying here with Mummy, would you?'

And Teddy Robinson said, 'No, I don't mind. I don't care about skipping myself, but you go. I'll watch you.'

So Deborah ran off to join the other children on the grass, and Teddy Robinson and Mummy stayed sitting on the seat in the sunshine.

Soon a lady came along, holding a very little boy by the hand. As soon as she saw Mummy the lady said, 'Oh, how nice to meet you here!' And she sat down beside her and started talking, because she was a friend of hers.

The very little boy, whose name was James, stared hard and said nothing.

'Look, James, this is Teddy Robinson,' said Mummy.

—rather dull together—

'Perhaps you would like to sit up beside him and talk to him.'

So James climbed up on the seat, and he and Teddy Robinson sat side by side and looked at each other, but neither of them said a word. They were both rather shy.

Mummy and the lady talked and talked and were very jolly together, but James and Teddy Robinson sat and did nothing and were rather dull together. After a while James grew tired of sitting still, so he climbed down off the seat, and when nobody was looking he lifted Teddy Robinson down too, and toddled away with him.

'I hope you aren't going to lose us,' said Teddy Robinson. But James said nothing at all.

They hadn't gone far before they came to some trees, and on the other side of the trees they saw a bandstand with rows of chairs all round it. It was like a little round summer-house, with open sides and a roof on top.

James and Teddy Robinson went over to look at it, and, as there was nobody there, they were able to go right up the steps and look inside. After that they ran in and out along the rows of empty chairs, until they came to the back row, just under the trees. Then James sat Teddy Robinson down on one of the chairs, and sat himself down on the one next to him.

'I'm glad I've got a chair to myself,' said Teddy Robinson. 'It would be a pity to share one when there are so many.'

But James didn't like sitting still for long. A moment later he got up again, and, forgetting all about Teddy Robinson, he ran back to the seat where Mummy and the lady were still talking. He was only a very little boy.

Teddy Robinson didn't mind at all. He felt rather grand sitting there all by himself on a chair of his own, with rows and rows of empty chairs standing all round him, and he began to think how nice it would be if some-one should happen to pass by and notice him.

He looked up into the leafy branches over his head, so that people would think he was just sitting there thinking, and wouldn't guess that he had really been left there by mistake. And then he began thinking of all

—just sitting there thinking

the things that people might say to each other when they
saw him.

> 'Look over there!
> Look where?
> Why, there.
> Take care, don't stare,
> but alone on that chair
> there's a teddy bear!
> I do declare!
> A bear on a chair
> with his head in the air!
> How *did* he get there?'

He said this to himself several times over, and then he went on:

> 'You can see that he's thinking
> (not preening or prinking,
> or winking or blinking,
> or prowling or slinking,
> or eating or drinking),
> but just sitting thinking . . .'

But he didn't think this was very good, and anyway he was getting into rather a muddle with so much thinking about thinking. So he was quite pleased when suddenly there was a rustling in the leaves over his head, and a sparrow hopped along the branch nearest to him and stared down at him with bright, beady eyes.

'Good afternoon,' chirped the sparrow. 'Are you waiting for the music?'

'Good afternoon,' said Teddy Robinson. 'What music?'

'The band,' said the sparrow. 'I thought perhaps you had come to sing with the band. It always plays here in the afternoons.'

'Oh,' said Teddy Robinson, 'how very nice that will be! I love singing.'

'So do I,' chirped the sparrow. 'We all do. There are quite a lot of us up in this tree, and we sing with the band every afternoon. I really don't know how they would manage without us. I'm sure people would miss us if we didn't join in.'

'How very jolly!' said Teddy Robinson. 'When will the music begin?'

"Are you waiting for the music?"

'Oh, very soon now,' said the sparrow. 'You'll see the chairs will soon begin to fill up, and then the band will arrive. Have you paid for your chair?'

'Oh, no,' said Teddy Robinson. 'Do I have to pay? I don't really want to buy it, only to sit in it for a little while.'

'Yes, but you have to pay just to sit in it,' said the sparrow. 'The ticket-man will be along in a minute. You'd better pretend to be asleep.'

But Teddy Robinson was far too excited to pretend to be asleep. He was longing for the band to come and for the music to begin.

Before long one or two people came along and sat

down in chairs near by; then two or three more people came, and after that more and more, until nearly all the rows of chairs were full. Several people looked as if they were just going to sit down in Teddy Robinson's chair, but they saw him just in time and moved on.

Then along came the ticket-man. Teddy Robinson began to feel rather worried when he saw all the people giving him money for their seats. But it was quite all right; the man came up to where he was sitting and stopped for a moment, then he smiled at Teddy Robinson and said, 'I suppose it's no use asking *you* to buy a ticket,' and went away.

Teddy Robinson was very glad.

'Was it all right?' asked the sparrow, peeping through the leaves.

'Yes,' said Teddy Robinson. 'I don't know how he knew I hadn't any money, but it's very nice for me, because now everyone will think I paid for my chair.'

He sat up straighter than ever, and started to have a little think about how nice it was, to be sitting in a chair and looking as though you'd paid for it:

> 'Look at that bear!
> He's paid for a chair;
> no wonder he looks so grand;
> with his paws in his lap,
> what a sensible chap!
> He's waiting to hear the band.'

And then the band arrived. The men wore red and gold uniforms, and they climbed up the steps to the bandstand, carrying their trumpets and flutes and a great big drum.

'Here they come!' chirped the sparrow from the tree. 'I must go and make sure the birds are all ready to start singing. Don't forget to join in yourself if you feel like it. Do you sing bass?'

'I don't know what that means,' said Teddy Robinson.

'Rather deep and growly,' said the sparrow.

'Oh, yes, I think perhaps I do,' said Teddy Robinson.

'Good,' said the sparrow. 'We birds all sing soprano (that means rather high and twittery). We could do with a good bass voice.' And he flew back into the tree again.

Then the band began to play.

The music went so fast that at first Teddy Robinson hadn't time to think of any words for it, so he just hummed happily to himself, and felt as if both he and the chair were jigging up and down in time to the music. Even the flies and bees began buzzing, and the birds were chirping so merrily, and the band was playing so loudly, that soon Teddy Robinson found some words to sing after all. They went like this:

> 'Trill-trill-trill
> goes the man with the flute,
> and the man with the trumpet
> goes toot-toot-toot.
> Cheep-cheep-cheep
> go the birds in the trees,
> and buzz-buzz-buzz
> go the flies and the bees.

Then the band began to play.

Mmmm-mmmm-mmmm
goes the teddy bear's hum,
and boom-boom-boom
goes the big bass drum.'

When the music stopped everyone clapped hard; but Teddy Robinson didn't clap, because, as he had been singing with the band, he was afraid it might look as if he were clapping himself.

He was just wondering whether he ought to get up and bow, as the leader of the band was doing, when he suddenly saw Deborah walking along between the rows of chairs.

She *was* surprised when she saw Teddy Robinson sitting among all the grown-up people.

'*However* did you get here?' she said. 'And why didn't I know? And fancy you having a chair all to yourself!'

'What a pity you didn't come before!' said Teddy Robinson. 'I've just been singing with the band. Did you hear everyone clapping?'

'Yes,' said Deborah, 'but I'd no idea they were clapping for you. I thought it was for the band.'

'Me *and* the band,' said Teddy Robinson, 'and the sparrows as well. They've been singing quite beautifully.'

'I *am* sorry I missed it,' said Deborah. 'I was skipping with the other children when somebody said the band had come, and I came over to see. I thought you were still sitting on the seat with Mummy.'

'James and I got tired of it,' said Teddy Robinson,

'so we came over here, and then James went back, so I stayed by myself. But you haven't missed all of it. Let's stay together and hear some more.'

Then Teddy Robinson moved up so that Deborah could share his chair.

'I do think you're a clever bear,' she said. 'I always knew you could sing very nicely, but I never thought I should find you singing with a proper band, and with everyone clapping you!'

And that is the end of the story about Teddy Robinson and the band.

8

Teddy Robinson and the
Beautiful Present

ONE day Teddy Robinson and Deborah went to
Granny's house for the afternoon.

After tea Granny gave Deborah a little round tin, full
of soapy stuff, and a piece of bent wire, round at one
end and straight at the other end.

'What is it for?' asked Deborah.

'It's for blowing bubbles,' said Granny. 'I'll show
you how to do it.' And she dipped the end of the wire
into the tin, and then blew gently through it into the
air. A whole stream of bubbles flew out into the
room.

'Oh!' exclaimed Deborah. 'What a Beautiful Present!'

'It will keep you happy till Daddy comes to fetch
you,' said Granny, and she went away to tidy up the tea
things.

Teddy Robinson sat in Granny's arm-chair and
watched Deborah blowing the bubbles. They were very
pretty.

'Can I have one?' he asked.

Deborah blew a bubble at him, and it landed on his
arm.

'Oh, thank you,' he said. 'Can I keep it?'

— they landed all over him —

But before Deborah could say yes, the bubble had made a tiny little splutter and burst.

'Well, I'm blowed!' said Teddy Robinson. 'That one's gone. Blow me another!'

So Deborah blew another. This one landed on his foot. But again it spluttered and burst.

'More!' said Teddy Robinson. So Deborah blew a whole stream of bubbles, and they landed all over him: one on his ear, one on his toe, five or six on his arms and legs, and one on the very end of his nose. But, one by one, they all spluttered and burst. Teddy Robinson's fur was damp where the bubbles had been, and he felt rather cross.

'The ones you give me aren't any good,' he said. 'They all burst.'

'They are meant to burst,' said Deborah.

'Then what's the good of them?' said Teddy Robinson.

'Just to look beautiful, for a minute,' said Deborah.

'I think that's silly,' said Teddy Robinson. 'If I couldn't look beautiful for more than a minute, without bursting, I wouldn't bother to look beautiful at all. Stop blowing bubbles and play with me instead.'

'No,' said Deborah. 'I can play with you any time. I want to play with my beautiful bubbles just now. Don't bother me, there's a good boy.'

So Teddy Robinson sat and sang to himself while he watched Deborah blowing bubbles.

'The trouble
with a bubble
is the way it isn't there
the minute that you've blown it
and thrown it
in the air.
It's a pity,
when you're pretty,
to disappear in air.
I'm glad I'm not a bubble;
I'd rather be a bear.'

When it was time to go home Daddy came to fetch them on his bicycle. Deborah ran to show him the Beautiful Present.

'Show me how it works when we get home,' said Daddy. 'We must hurry now, because Mummy is waiting for us.'

So Teddy Robinson and Deborah said good-bye to Granny, and Daddy took them out to the front gate where his bicycle was waiting. He popped Teddy Robinson into the basket on the front, then he lifted Deborah up into the little seat at the back, just behind him.

'You carry my Beautiful Present, Daddy,' said Deborah. So Daddy put it in his pocket. Then off they all went.

Teddy Robinson loved riding in the bicycle basket. The wind whistled in his fur, and he sang to himself all the way home:

> 'Head over heels,
> how nice it feels,
> a basket-y ride
> on bicycle wheels.'

It was beginning to get dark, and the lights were going on in all the houses when at last they reached home.

'Now run in quickly,' said Daddy, as he lifted Deborah down from her little seat. 'Here are your bubbles,' he said, and he took Granny's present out of his pocket.

Deborah ran in at the front door where Mummy was waiting. Teddy Robinson heard her calling as she ran, 'Look, Mummy – I've got such a Beautiful Present!' Then the front door shut behind them.

Daddy wheeled the bicycle round the side of the house to the tool-shed. He opened the door and pushed the bicycle inside, leaning it up against the wall. Then he went out again and shut the door behind him.

'Oh, dear!' said Teddy Robinson. 'They've forgotten I'm still in the basket. I expect they'll come back and fetch me later.'

But they didn't come back and fetch him, because Daddy had quite forgotten that he had put Teddy Robinson in the basket, and Deborah thought she must have left him at Granny's house. So she went to bed thinking that Granny would be bringing him back to-morrow.

It was very dark in the tool-shed, and very quiet.

Teddy Robinson smoothed his fur and pulled up his braces, and sang a little song to keep himself company:

> 'Oh, my fur and braces!
> How dark it is at night
> sitting in the tool-shed
> without electric light!
>
> 'Sitting in the tool-shed,
> with no one here but me.
> Oh, my fur and braces,
> what a funny place to be!'

He rather liked the bit about the fur and braces, so he sang it again. Then he stopped singing and listened to the quietness instead. And after a while he found that it wasn't really quiet at all in the tool-shed. All sorts of little noises and rustlings were going on, very tiny little noises that he wouldn't have noticed if everything else hadn't been so quiet.

94

—it hung just in front of his nose

First he heard the bustling of a lot of little earwigs running to and fro under a pile of logs in the corner. Then he heard the panting of a crowd of tiny ants who were struggling across the floor with a long twig they were carrying. Then he heard the sigh of a little moth as it shook its wings and fluttered about the windowpane. Teddy Robinson was glad to think he wasn't all by himself in the tool-shed after all.

Suddenly something came dropping down from the ceiling on a long, thin thread and hung just in front of his nose. It made one or two funny faces at him, then pulled itself up again and disappeared out of sight.

Teddy Robinson was so frightened that he nearly fell out of the bicycle basket. But then he realized that it was only a spider.

What a pity, he thought. I'd have said Good Evening if I'd known it was coming.

A moment later he felt a gentle plop on top of his head and knew that the spider had come down again. This time he wasn't frightened, only surprised.

It seemed rather silly to say Good Evening to someone who was sitting on top of his head, so Teddy Robinson began singing again, in his smallest voice, just to let the spider know he was there.

> 'Oh, my fur and braces!
> You did give me a fright,
> making funny faces
> in the middle of the night!
>
> 'Hanging from the ceiling
> by a tiny silver thread,
> what a funny feeling
> when you landed on my head!'

The spider crawled across the front of Teddy Robinson's head and looked down into one of his eyes.

'I say!' he said. 'I do beg your pardon. I didn't know it was your head I'd landed on. And when I came down the first time I'd no idea I was making faces at you. I was simply looking for somewhere to spin a web. I'm sorry I frightened you.'

'That's all right,' said Teddy Robinson.

'I believe I do make funny faces when I'm thinking,' said the spider. 'I often seem to frighten people without meaning to. Have you heard about Miss Muffet? Well, I gave her such a fright that they've been making a song about it ever since; but it was quite by mistake, you know.'

Teddy Robinson began to feel rather sorry for the spider who was always frightening people without meaning to, so he said, 'Well, *I'm* not frightened of you. I'm pleased to see you.'

'Have you come to live here?' asked the spider.

'Oh, I hope not,' said Teddy Robinson. 'I mean I'm really only here by mistake. Deborah's sure to come and find me in the morning. She wouldn't have forgotten me tonight if she hadn't been given a Beautiful Present.'

'What was it?' asked the spider.

'Bubbles,' said Teddy Robinson. 'They were very pretty, but they kept bursting.'

'And did you have a Beautiful Present too?'

'No,' said Teddy Robinson sadly.

'What a shame,' said the spider. 'You know, I could make you a Beautiful Present myself. It wouldn't last very long, but it would last longer than a bubble.'

'Could you really?' said Teddy Robinson.

'Yes,' said the spider. 'I could spin a web for you. I make rather beautiful webs, and they look lovely with the light shining on them.'

'Oh, thank you,' said Teddy Robinson. 'I should like that. Will I be able to take it away with me?'

'Yes,' said the spider. 'but I must be careful not to join it to the wall or it will break when you move.'

'And don't join it to the bicycle basket either, will you?' said Teddy Robinson. 'I don't usually live in that.'

'I see,' said the spider. 'Well, I will start at your ear, and go down here, and along here, and I'll catch the thread to your foot if you're sure that doesn't tickle you?'

'Yes, that will be very nice,' said Teddy Robinson. 'Shall I sing to you while you work?'

'Oh, do,' said the spider. 'I love music while I work.'

So Teddy Robinson began singing:

'Spin, little spider, spin,
in and out and in.'

And as he sang he heard a gentle whirring noise quite close to his ear, and knew that the spider had started spinning the web that was to be his Beautiful Present.

Soon the gentle noise of the spider spinning made Teddy Robinson so drowsy that he forgot to sing any more, and a little while afterwards he fell fast asleep.

It was morning when he woke up again. Someone was just opening the tool-shed door, and as the sunshine came streaming in Teddy Robinson could see the silver thread of the spider's web reaching right down to his toes. He kept very still so as not to break it.

Daddy had come to fetch his bicycle. As soon as he saw Teddy Robinson he called Deborah. She *was* surprised to see him.

—reaching right down *to his toes*

'I thought we'd left you at Granny's!' she said. 'Oh, you poor boy!'

'Yes, but look what he's got!' said Daddy.

'Oh, how lovely!' said Deborah, and she called Mummy to come and see. And Mummy and Daddy and Deborah all crowded round the bicycle to look at Teddy Robinson and admire his beautiful web.

'A spider must have made it in the night,' said Daddy.

'Look how it sparkles in the sun!' said Mummy.

'And Teddy Robinson has got a Beautiful Present all of his own!' said Deborah.

Then Teddy Robinson was lifted very carefully out of the bicycle basket, and Deborah carried him into the house, holding him in front of her with both hands, so as not to break a single thread of the web.

'What happened to *your* Beautiful Present?' asked Teddy Robinson.

'It's finished. I threw away the tin,' said Deborah.

'And where are all the bubbles?'

'Gone,' said Deborah. 'They all burst. Your web won't last for ever either. Nothing does.'

'Except me,' said Teddy Robinson. 'It's a good thing *I* don't burst, isn't it?'

And that is the end of the story about Teddy Robinson and the Beautiful Present.

9

Teddy Robinson and Guy Fawkes

ONE wintry afternoon Teddy Robinson was sitting under the dining-room table. He was all alone. Deborah had been playing houses with him until Mummy had sent her off to Andrew's house to invite him to her party on Saturday.

Teddy Robinson knew all about the party. He was looking forward to it a lot, because it was going to be a fireworks party, and Teddy Robinson loved things that went off with a bang. He began singing a little song about it to himself while he waited for Deborah to come back.

> 'Fireworks are coming,
> hooray, hooray.
> Fireworks are coming
> on Saturday.
> Hold your ears
> and hide your eyes.
> BANG, BANG, BANG!
> What a nice surprise!'

Teddy Robinson stopped singing and listened. He could hear Mummy and Daddy talking together in the kitchen.

'Where's Deborah?' said Daddy. 'I thought we might make a guy. Have you got some old clothes and newspapers?'

'Oh, yes,' said Mummy. 'Deborah's gone to Andrew's house. I expect she's stayed to play with him. But let's go and see what we can find.'

'Now, I wonder whatever they're talking about,' said Teddy Robinson to himself. But he couldn't guess, because he didn't know what a guy was.

For a long time he could hear them talking and laughing together in the kitchen, but after a while he got tired of wondering what they were doing and dozed off to sleep instead.

He woke up with a start. Someone had just opened the door. Teddy Robinson peeped out from under the table and saw Daddy coming in with the funniest-looking man he had ever seen. Daddy sat the funny-looking man down on the floor and propped him up against the table-leg.

'There you are, old boy,' he said. 'You just wait till Deborah sees you!' Then he went out again and shut the door.

Teddy Robinson had a good look at the funny man.

He was wearing a very old coat of Daddy's, and a very old hat of Mummy's, and some very old leggings of Deborah's. His hair, sticking out from under Mummy's old hat, looked as if it was made of straw, and he had a funny, laughing face which looked just as though it had been painted on cardboard.

'Whoever are you?' said Teddy Robinson.

The funny man looked sideways at him. Then he laughed, and a strange noise of rustling newspapers came from inside his jacket.

"Whoever are you?"

'Fancy not knowing who *I* am!' he said.

'*I'm* Guy Fawkes, sir.
How do you do?
I'm Guy Fawkes, sir.
Who are you?'

'I'm Teddy Robinson. How do you do? May I ask what you're doing here? And why are you wearing my family's clothes?'

'Your family was kind enough to lend them to me,' said Guy Fawkes. 'I've come for the party.'

'But the party isn't until Saturday,' said Teddy Robinson.

'I know,' said the guy; 'but I like to be ready in plenty of time.'

103

'I never heard of anyone coming to a party two whole days early,' said Teddy Robinson. 'Where are you going to stay?'

'Here, of course,' said the guy. 'It's only two days to wait. A short life but a merry one, eh? Ha, ha, ha!'

He laughed again with a great crackling of newspapers, and his hat slipped a little bit sideways on his head.

Teddy Robinson couldn't see anything to laugh at. He didn't much like the idea of this funny-looking man coming to live in his house. But the guy seemed to be a jolly fellow, so Teddy Robinson tried to be friendly and make him feel at home.

'We're going to have a lovely lot of fireworks on Saturday,' he said.

'Good,' said the guy. 'There's nothing I like better. And will there be a lot of children here?'

'Oh, yes,' said Teddy Robinson. 'Deborah's gone to invite one of them now. I expect she'll be home soon.'

And at that minute Deborah came running in from Andrew's house. When she saw the guy sitting on the dining-room floor she laughed and clapped her hands.

'Daddy told me he was here,' she said.

Teddy Robinson said. 'This is Mr Spoons. He says he's come to stay. He came while you were out.'

Deborah laughed more than ever.

'He's not Mr Spoons,' she said, 'he's Mr Fawkes and he hasn't come to stay. He's come to be burnt on the bonfire.'

Teddy Robinson was very surprised to hear Deborah

say this. It didn't seem at all a polite thing to say about a visitor. But the guy didn't seem to mind. He just went on smiling all the time.

When bedtime came Teddy Robinson was very glad to find that the guy wasn't going to share their bed with them. He was quite happy to be left in the kitchen, propped up in a corner by the back door. So Teddy Robinson was able to ask Deborah if it was really true that he was going to be burnt on the bonfire at the party.

'Oh, yes,' said Deborah. 'That is what guys are for. Aren't we lucky to have such a fine one?'

But Teddy Robinson was beginning to feel rather sorry for the guy.

All the next day the guy stood in the corner of the kitchen, grinning happily at everyone as they came in and out. Teddy Robinson had a little talk with him once when they were left on their own.

'Do you like being you?' he asked. 'You smile such a lot anybody'd think you enjoyed it.'

'Oh, but I do,' said the guy. 'Don't you like being you?'

'Yes, thank you,' said Teddy Robinson. 'I like it very much. I was only thinking . . .' But he didn't know how to finish what he was saying, because he was thinking about what was going to happen to the guy on Saturday.

'I was thinking about the fireworks party,' he said.

'So was I,' said the guy. 'I'm looking forward to it no end – aren't you?'

'Well, yes, I am,' said Teddy Robinson; 'but

"Do you like being you?"

somehow I didn't expect a guy to. I saw one today at the shops being wheeled in a pushchair by a little boy, and I thought he looked rather sad.'

'Oh, those guys in pushchairs!' said the guy. 'I don't even count them; they're hardly guys at all. They haven't even got enough stuffing in them to sit up straight. And no wonder they look sad! They have to sit there for hours while the boys shout, "Penny for the guy, mister!" Well, no decent guy would like to sit there listening to children begging for him, would he? Surely you don't think I look like one of them, do you?'

'Oh, no,' said Teddy Robinson; 'I think you're the finest guy I ever met, I really do.'

Saturday came at last, and everybody was busy getting ready for the party. Deborah counted the fireworks over and over again. Mummy was busy making toffee-apples and scrubbing big potatoes to roast in the bonfire. Daddy made a huge pile of wood and old boxes down at the bottom of the garden.

But Teddy Robinson hung around feeling rather sad, and getting more and more worried about the guy. Did he know about the bonfire yet? He said he was looking forward to the party, so he *couldn't* know.

I wonder if I ought to tell him, thought Teddy Robinson.

'Why are you looking so sad?' asked Deborah. 'Aren't you looking forward to the fireworks?'

'I think perhaps I won't go to the party, after all,' said Teddy Robinson.

Just then Daddy came tramping in from the garden.

'Do take the guy outside,' said Mummy. 'He's in my way here.'

So Daddy carried the guy outside and propped him up against the wall by the dustbins.

'I want to go out there with him,' said Teddy Robinson.

'All right,' said Deborah, and she took him out and sat him beside the guy on one of the dustbins.

The guy leaned up against the wall and looked down at Teddy Robinson with a great big, jolly smile.

'Well, well,' he said, 'it's the great day at last! Why so sad? Aren't you looking forward to the party?'

'Not much. I don't think I'm coming.'

107

'Of course you're coming!' said the guy. 'Look here, I've just thought of something! Are you going to have a bonfire of your own?'

'How do you mean?' said Teddy Robinson.

'Well, they're not going to burn you on *my* bonfire, are they? It wouldn't be fair. There isn't room for two of us, and I don't want to share my bonfire with anybody.'

'I'm not going to be burnt on any bonfire,' said Teddy Robinson.

'Oh, bad luck!' said the guy. 'No wonder you look sad!'

'But I don't *want* to be burnt on a bonfire,' said Teddy Robinson. 'Do you mean you really don't mind?'

'What a funny chap you are!' said the guy. 'Why, I've been looking forward to it ever since I came. Every guy does. It's the big minute of his life. When the flames go shooting up all round me, and I start crackling and burning, I shall be the finest sight in the garden. Are you sure you're not jealous? You *must* come and watch me, or I shall know you're jealous, and that will spoil my finest minute.'

Teddy Robinson was so pleased to hear the guy say this that he began looking forward to the party all over again.

'Of course I'll come,' he said. 'I wouldn't miss it for anything.'

'That's a good fellow,' said the guy.

So at half-past four, when all the children came, Teddy Robinson was just as excited as Deborah.

As soon as it was dark and tea was over they all put on their coats and ran out into the garden. Teddy Robinson, with a scarf tied round his neck, sat on the step by the garden door. Deborah gave him a sparkler all his own. He was very pleased.

'But I won't hold it,' he said. 'It might burn my paws.'

So Deborah stuck the sparkler into some earth in a flower-pot and put it in front of him on the step.

'There,' she said, 'that is your very own firework.'

'Will you light it before you burn the guy?' said Teddy Robinson. 'I'd like him to see it before he goes.'

'Yes,' said Deborah. 'Let's go and have a look at him now.'

So they went down the garden to have a last look at the guy before Daddy set light to the bonfire.

He was standing right on top of the pile, smiling all over his face and staring up at the stars.

'Hallo,' said Teddy Robinson. 'I've just come to say good-bye. And I wanted to tell you, I've got a firework all of my own. Watch out for it. It'll be the very first sparkler.'

'I'll watch!' said the guy. 'Jolly good show!' Then, as the other children all crowded round to admire him, the guy lurched a little sideways and whispered:

'Jolly nice of you to come and watch me, old boy. Never mind – your turn will come one day.'

'Now stand back, all of you!' said Daddy. 'I'm just going to light the bonfire.'

'Wait!' cried Deborah. 'Teddy Robinson's got to have his sparkler first. I promised him.'

*— smiling all over his face
and staring up at the stars —*

All the children ran to the step and stood round waiting to see Teddy Robinson's firework lighted. He felt very proud. But when it suddenly burst out spluttering he was so surprised that he rolled over backward and fell off the step. Deborah sat him up again, and he watched proudly until the last little silver star had died away. Teddy Robinson thought it was the finest firework he had ever seen.

After that Daddy lit the bonfire, and while the flames crept slowly upward he let off rockets, and Catherine-wheels, and jumping crackers; and all the children shouted 'O-o-o-oh!' every time a new one went off.

The bonfire roared and blazed and crackled at the end of the garden. Teddy Robinson could see the guy's

the finest firework he had ever seen

proud and happy smile lit up by the bright flames until at last he was all burnt up.

The fireworks went *Bang, Crackle, Swish, Pop,* until Teddy Robinson could hardly hear himself thinking. And so many coloured stars and flares went shooting up into the sky that he didn't even know which way his eyes were looking.

Soon the garden was filled with the most delicious smell of gunpowder, and much later on with an even more delicious smell of roast potatoes. It was a wonderful party. It seemed to go on for hours and hours.

When at last it was over and the children had all gone

home Deborah came to fetch Teddy Robinson to bed. She found him lying flat on his back on the step, staring up at the sky, and singing softly to the stars:

'Splutter, splutter, sparkle,
what a jolly sight!
Did you see my firework
exploding in the night?

'Splutter, crackle, BANG,
from six o'clock till nine,
fifty million fireworks,
but none as fine as mine!'

Soon Teddy Robinson was tucked up in bed beside Deborah, his sleepy head still full of swishing stars and surprises.

He was just dropping off to sleep when he suddenly remembered the very last thing the guy had said to him, 'Never mind – your turn will come one day.'

Teddy Robinson woke up with a start.

'It won't, will it?' he said out loud to Deborah.

'What won't, will it?' said Deborah sleepily.

'My turn won't come, will it?' said Teddy Robinson. 'I won't be burnt on a bonfire, will I?'

'Good gracious, no!' said Deborah. 'What ever made you think of that?'

And that is the end of the story about Teddy Robinson and Guy Fawkes.

10

Teddy Robinson Goes Magic

ONE day Teddy Robinson was sitting in the garden under the apple-tree when all of a sudden a large rosy apple fell with a *plop*, right in the middle of his lap.

'Who threw that?' said Teddy Robinson, but no one answered because there was nobody there to answer. Teddy Robinson was all by himself in the garden.

'How very surprising,' he said to himself. 'Fancy it coming just like that, out of nowhere!' And then he had a sudden idea. 'My goodness!' he said to himself. 'Have I gone magic?'

Teddy Robinson thought how very exciting it would be if he had gone magic, but he couldn't be sure yet. He waited to see if anything else was going to happen. While he was waiting he looked at the rosy apple lying in his lap.

'I should like to have a large hat,' he said to himself, 'with apples like this growing all round it. Mrs Grey

113

I should like to have a large hat

with apples growing all round it

next door has a large hat with flowers growing all round it. I wish I had a hat like Mrs Grey's.'

Just then there was a sudden gust of wind, and a large hat with flowers all round it came floating over the wall and landed right at Teddy Robinson's feet.

Teddy Robinson could hardly believe it.

'Why, this is just like Mrs Grey's hat!' he said. 'I wished for a hat like Mrs Grey's, and now it has come, all by itself. What a pity I forgot to say I wanted apples, round mine instead of flowers. But never mind, I'm sure this will suit me just as well. And *how* exciting, I really must be magic!'

Teddy Robinson was quite excited. He began singing to himself:

> 'Abracadabra,
> magic me,
> underneath the apple-tree.

Abracadabra,
fancy that!
I wished myself a magic hat.
and down it came
just floating on air,
a magic hat for a magic bear!'

Then he began thinking of all the things he might be able to do now that he was magic.

I will do something really big for Deborah, he thought. Now, I wonder what she would like. What's the biggest thing I can think of?

He thought hard for a minute. Then he said, 'I know! An elephant. I can't think of anything bigger than that. I'll order an elephant for Deborah. She would love to have rides round the garden on it. I wonder where they'll keep it, though. Oh, how I wish someone was here to talk to about it!'

At that very minute the next-door kitten came scampering through the grass and trotted up to Teddy Robinson.

'Hallo,' said the kitten. 'I thought I might find you here. How are you?'

'Hallo,' said Teddy Robinson. He was so surprised that he couldn't think of anything else to say for a minute. He had forgotten, when he wished he had some-one to talk to, that he might be making another magic.

'What a pur-r-rfectly lovely day!' said the next-door kitten. 'I've been chasing leaves in the garden. This wind gets in my fur and makes me feel so frisky. What have you been doing?'

"I can do magic too. Look at this!"

'I have been doing magic,' said Teddy Robinson. 'I wished for you to come.'

'Did you really?' purred the next-door kitten. 'That was very sweet of you.'

'I don't mean that,' said Teddy Robinson. 'I mean I've been doing magic.'

'I can do magic too,' said the next-door kitten. 'Look at this!' And she arched up her back and went *S-s-s-s!* and all her fur stood up on end so that her tail looked like a brush.

'That's very clever,' said Teddy Robinson, 'but that's not magic.'

'And I can make my eyes shine in the dark,' said the next-door kitten.

'That's nothing,' said Teddy Robinson. 'I can make apples fall into my lap and magic hats come from nowhere. Look at this. Don't you think it's rather fine?'

The next-door kitten walked all round the hat, sniffing at the flowers with her eyes shut.

'They don't smell,' she said, 'but it's a very fine hat, for all that. Are you going to wear it?'

'I shall wait till Deborah comes,' said Teddy Robinson. 'She is good at trying things on me. What I really want to talk to you about is the elephant.'

The next-door kitten looked very surprised.

'What elephant?' she said.

'I am going to wish for an elephant for Deborah,' said Teddy Robinson. 'I want to give her a really big surprise, and that is the biggest thing I can think of. The only thing that's worrying me is where she will keep it.'

Just then there was a pattering of raindrops in the leaves of the apple-tree overhead.

'Oh, dear!' said the next-door kitten. 'It's beginning to rain. What a pity! I'm afraid I shall have to go. I mustn't get my paws wet.' And she scampered off.

At the same minute Deborah came running out of the house calling, 'Come in, Teddy Robinson. It's raining.'

She was very surprised when she saw the apple in his lap and the flowery hat lying at his feet.

'Wherever did you get these?' she asked as she carried them all indoors.

'I got them by magic,' said Teddy Robinson. 'You can have the apple, but the hat is for me. It's a magic hat. Will you try it on me and see if it fits?'

'I think it's miles too big for you,' said Deborah, but she sat him down on the dining-room table and put the

It is rather big, but it's nice and shady

hat on his head, just to make sure. Then she started laughing, because the hat was so big that it covered the whole of Teddy Robinson's head and face. But Teddy Robinson didn't laugh at all.

'It is rather large,' he said, 'but it's nice and shady. I think I'll keep it on for a little while. I ought to be able to do some really good magic under a hat as large as this.'

But Deborah just went on laughing and laughing.

'I don't know how it managed to get into our garden,' she said, 'but I'm sure it must be Mrs Grey's hat, because you look just like Mrs Grey with it on. I wish you could see how funny you look.'

'You don't laugh at Mrs Grey when she is wearing her hat,' said Teddy Robinson; 'so why do you laugh at me? I think it is very rude of you. I was going to make a nice big surprise for you, but I shan't if you don't stop laughing. Please go away.'

'All right,' said Deborah. 'I'll go and tell Mummy about it.'

Deborah went away, and Teddy Robinson stayed sitting on the dining-room table under the magic hat. He began thinking about the wish he was going to make for Deborah's elephant.

'I may as well do it now,' he said to himself, 'before anyone comes and interrupts me.'

It was such a very large wish that Teddy Robinson wasn't quite sure how to make it. So he pretended to himself that he was in a large shop where you could order a wish just as you might order anything else. He said, 'Good morning,' to himself in a polite voice, and then he said,

'I wish for an elephant.
– *pink or blue?* –
No, black or white,
or grey will do.

'I wish for an elephant.
– *yes, what size?* –
As large as can be,
for a big surprise.

'I wish for an elephant.
– *yes, how soon?* –
Please send it along
this afternoon.'

Then he said, 'Thank you very much,' to himself, and waited to see what would happen.

There was a ring at the front-door bell. Teddy Robinson held his breath and listened. A minute later Deborah came running into the room.

"Has the elephant come?"

'Has the elephant come?' asked Teddy Robinson.

'The elephant?' said Deborah, surprised. 'Whatever do you mean? No, that was Mrs Grey. She came to ask if her hat had blown over the wall into our garden, and I said yes, it had. I've come to fetch it now.' And she took the big flowery hat off Teddy Robinson's head and ran out into the hall again.

Poor Teddy Robinson! He felt very small and ordinary without his beautiful magic hat; and he felt very cross with Deborah because she had laughed at him when he was wearing it, and now she had come and taken it away.

'I shan't talk to her at all when she comes back,' he said to himself.

So when Deborah came running back a few minutes later, saying, 'Teddy Robinson, I've got something lovely to tell you,' he took no notice at all and pretended not to hear.

'What's the matter!' said Deborah. 'Why don't you want to listen?'

'I'm cross with you,' said Teddy Robinson, 'because you laughed at me, and now you've taken away my magic hat. Anybody'd think you'd be pleased to have a bear who was magic.'

'But it isn't your hat. It's Mrs Grey's,' said Deborah. 'And what makes you think you're magic?'

'Well, aren't I?'

'N), I don't think so,' said Deborah. 'You're quite the nicest teddy bear I've ever met, but you're not *magic*. Why should you be?'

Then Teddy Robinson told her all about how the apple had fallen out of nowhere into his lap.

'But it didn't fall out of nowhere,' said Deborah. 'It fell out of the tree because it was ripe.'

Teddy Robinson thought about this.

'But what about the hat?' he said. 'It just came floating over the wall. Didn't my magic do that?'

'Of course not,' said Deborah. 'The wind made that happen.'

Then Teddy Robinson told her about how he wished he had someone to talk to, and the next-door kitten had come running up.

'Well, I expect she was just playing in the garden and saw you there,' said Deborah. 'She's a friendly little kitten.'

'But didn't I do *anything*?' asked Teddy Robinson.

Deborah thought hard. 'Yes,' she said, 'you sat in the garden and you saw the hat blow over the wall; and when I came out to fetch you I found it; and now Mrs Grey is so pleased because we took it into the house when it started raining that she's asked me to go to the Zoo with her this afternoon.'

'*Has* she?' said Teddy Robinson. 'What did she say?'

'She said, "Thank you very much for looking after my hat so nicely," and then she said, "How would you like a ride on an elephant this afternoon? I'm taking my little grandson to the Zoo, and perhaps you would like to come with us?"'

'Well,' said Teddy Robinson, 'you may be right about the apple, and the hat, and the kitten, but do you know I *wished* for you to have an elephant? Yes, I truly did, while I was under the magic hat, and now you're going to have one.'

'I'm going to have a ride on one,' said Deborah. 'I'm not sure if that's quite the same thing, but thank you for such a nice wish.'

'I'm glad you like it,' said Teddy Robinson. 'That was the big surprise I was making for you. The only thing that worried me was where we were going to keep it. I think it's a jolly good idea to keep it in the Zoo. I don't know why I didn't think of it myself. Can I come with you this afternoon?'

'Of course you can,' said Deborah. 'That's what I came to tell you. We'll both go for a ride on my elephant. How clever of you to think of it! You know, I think you may be right. Perhaps you are a tiny little bit magic after all!'

And that is the end of the story about how Teddy Robinson went magic.

Also in Young Puffin

Joan G. Robinson

DEAR TEDDY
ROBINSON

**Classic stories about a charming teddy bear,
loved for many years by generations
of readers.**

In these eight delightful tales, perfect for reading
aloud to young children, Teddy Robinson pays a
visit to the Dolls' Hospital, gets stuck up a tree,
pretends to be a polar bear and lots more.

Joan G. Robinson

KEEPING UP WITH TEDDY ROBINSON

**Classic stories about a charming teddy bear,
loved for many years by generations
of readers.**

In this book, perfect for reading aloud to young
children, Teddy Robinson helps some fieldmice
move house, finds himself in the park litter bin
and is sold by mistake in a jumble sale!

READ MORE IN PUFFIN

For children of all ages, Puffin represents quality and variety – the very best in publishing today around the world.

For complete information about books available from Puffin – and Penguin – and how to order them, contact us at the appropriate address below. Please note that for copyright reasons the selection of books varies from country to country.

On the worldwide web: www.puffin.co.uk

In the United Kingdom: Please write to *Dept. EP, Penguin Books Ltd, Bath Road, Harmondsworth, West Drayton, Middlesex UB7 0DA*

In the United States: Please write to *Consumer Sales, Penguin USA, P.O. Box 999, Dept. 17109, Bergenfield, New Jersey 07621-0120*. VISA and MasterCard holders call 1-800-253-6476 to order Penguin titles

In Canada: Please write to *Penguin Books Canada Ltd, 10 Alcorn Avenue, Suite 300, Toronto, Ontario M4V 3B2*

In Australia: Please write to *Penguin Books Australia Ltd, P.O. Box 257, Ringwood, Victoria 3134*

In New Zealand: Please write to *Penguin Books (NZ) Ltd, Private Bag 102902, North Shore Mail Centre, Auckland 10*

In India: Please write to *Penguin Books India Pvt Ltd, 706 Eros Apartments, 56 Nehru Place, New Delhi 110 019*

In the Netherlands: Please write to *Penguin Books Netherlands bv, Postbus 3507, NL-1001 AH Amsterdam*

In Germany: Please write to *Penguin Books Deutschland GmbH, Metzlerstrasse 26, 60594 Frankfurt am Main*

In Spain: Please write to *Penguin Books S. A., Bravo Murillo 19, 1° B, 28015 Madrid*

In Italy: Please write to *Penguin Italia s.r.l., Via Felice Casati 20, I–20124 Milano.*

In France: Please write to *Penguin France S. A., 17 rue Lejeune, F–31000 Toulouse*

In Japan: Please write to *Penguin Books Japan, Ishikiribashi Building, 2–5–4, Suido, Bunkyo-ku, Tokyo 112*

In South Africa: Please write to *Longman Penguin Southern Africa (Pty) Ltd, Private Bag X08, Bertsham 2013*